A MYSTERY OF CROSS WOMEN

Timberdick's First Case
Liking Good Jazz
Piggy Tucker's Poison
The Case of the Dirty Verger
The Parish of Frayed Ends

MALCOLM NOBLE

A Mystery of
Cross Women

Matador
9 De Montfort Mews
Leicester LE1 7FW, UK
Tel: 0116 255 9312
Email: matador@troubador.co.uk
Web: www.troubador.co.uk/matador

ISBN 978-1848760-929

This is a work of fiction. All characters and events are imaginary,
and any resemblance to actual persons and events is purely coincidental.

Typeset in 10.5pt Stempel Garamond by Troubador Publishing Ltd, Leicester, UK
Printed by the MPG Books Group in the UK

Matador is an imprint of Troubador Publishing Ltd

To Christine

AUTHOR'S NOTE

I hesitated before calling this story a Timberdick Mystery. The murder takes place in 1937. Timbers is seven years old and makes no more than a guest appearance in Chapter Four. Really, it is Ned's story. However, the background and several of the characters are familiar so I think it sits neatly into the saga.

Chronologically, A Mystery of Cross Women is the first episode.

PART ONE

THE TEN O'CLOCK MURDER

ONE

The Dean's Clerk

In the daytime, St Greg's stood like a father over the narrow lanes and leaning buildings in this part of our city. But Greg's after dark had more to do with scoundrels and skulduggery than the doings of honest neighbours. Good men and women had no business in the graveyard after ten.

At twenty minutes to, Hubert Wycherley, the Dean's Clerk, stood at the top of his three doorsteps and twisted around to check that his terraced cottage was properly locked. His nose twitched; the petty trawlers were in and the taste of salt and fishgut drifted up the crooked lanes from the quay. The smell was worse tonight because the air was close and, although the evening was warm enough for shirt sleeves, the Dean's Clerk wore a heavy black coat with broad pockets and a floppy black hat which he tugged at the front before alighting from the stone steps to the newly cobbled close.

He carried a leather manuscript satchel under one sleeve and, with every few steps, he held it closer to his chest and brought two gloved fingers to his lips to stall a fidgety cough. Hubert wasn't a nervous man but he had been studying hard and he didn't feel strong. And when he was tired, he coughed (a habit that schoolmasters had tried to beat out of him in the olden days). He was very satisfied with his evening's work. Two hours at his desk – a dimly lit scene with a shaded table lamp at a timber framed window that looked onto next door's brick wall – had brought together the product six of months observations along the coastline. Charts, columns of figures, angles drawn across tracing paper. Now, the people in charge could examine his evidence and make up their minds.

3

He cleared his throat and resettled the leather case in the crook of his elbow. "Other matters," he said quietly to himself. "Now we must talk of other matters."

The cathedral cat shrunk into her shoulders as the clerk's dark figure trod past the railings. Puss was up to no good and didn't want to be caught. She dithered for hardly a second, but the hesitation was sufficient for a captured vole to break from the cat's cruel claw. The rooks laughed wickedly as they circled the cathedral tower and a mongrel emerged from the cellar steps and trespassed freely, as if to show the cat that she wasn't as clever as she thought she was. But, being a wise old moggy, Puss kept her own counsel; the wretched vole was broken and bloody and could be easily caught again.

The rooks, the cat and the dog watched the clerk's grey shape sink into the murky twilight. Hubert paused at the crossroads and, beneath a dim streetlamp, he took out his pocket watch and checked it against the clock on the tower. He had always preached that the clock reflected the truth and dependability of our church. He said the same about the weather vane at the crown of the wrought iron gates and the compass in the bowl of the disused font that now stood in the cathedral garden.

He had timed his walk from Cathedral Close to the Palfreyman pub so that he could hear the 9.43 from Waterloo arrive at the town station. The lines took the trains higher than many of the surrounding roofs, so its arrival would be heard clearly on a quiet night like tonight. She was already late but Hubert could allow her a few minutes. The harbour mouth was less than a quarter of a mile away and, as he waited, he heard a lightly loaded freighter chugging through the channel to the spithead. It sounded like a very clean engine, as if the vessel moved by levers and chains rather than propellers. Hubert wasn't a scientific man but he liked the sounds of engines. He had always thought that paddles made the cleanest sound of all.

Two hundred yards up the High Street, a sergeant farrier and two privates were trying to coax a highly strung horse into the barrack's livery stables. Knowing their jobs, the soldiers had already called for Sidney the coalman to bring up his mare. This docile, hardworking beast of burden, content between the shafts of her coal wagon, would settle the army horse. Hubert stood and watched the whole adventure; then, at five to ten, he gave up on the London train and crossed the road.

On the other side of the junction, in another cobbled lane, a young man was working beneath the bonnet of an Austin Ten-Four. He had rigged a hurricane lamp above the engine and it swayed as he shifted his weight against the car's body. He had parked next to the Palfreyman so that he also had the light from the pub.

"Good evening Bert," he said without coming up from the engine.

The Dean's Clerk divided the world into two; men who called him Bert and men who did not.

"Do you think there'll be war?"

Not this year or next, Hubert wanted to say. But he kept quiet, largely because the mechanic had called him Bert and he wanted to be rude in return. He gave his music case an extra tug as he went through the black lacquered doors of the Palfreyman.

Rosie Ditchen and Mrs Ritchers were in the saloon and no-one else.

"Your two gentlemen are waiting upstairs," Mrs Ritchers said as Hubert took off his hat. Her remark was something of a joke, for everyone knew that Ernie Berkeley and Shaking Jacobs weren't gentlemen; they were neither well bred nor good mannered. (Jacobs worried too much and people called Berkeley 'Soapy'.) "You'll need to put your hat down, dear, or you won't be able to carry the tray." She had placed half a pint of beer, three loose cigarettes and a match on a wooden tray for him; Hubert had already picked up the beer.

He put down some halfpennies and said, "I'll drink with Rosie Ditchen first." He took the beer glass and the smokes but left the tray on the counter.

While the landlady looked smart, with a broach on the wide collar of her dress and an embroidered modesty vest to compensate for a deep neckline, her customer in the corner was all trussed up and dowdy. Wrapped in her woollen overcoat and rooted in well-padded ankle boots, Rosie Ditchen had the look of a compact woman, full of secrets. The colours on her face were always wrong. When she glowed, she was red in all the wrong places. And her ordinary complexion – a sort of chalky, pastry look – seemed to throw any

5

shadows askew. She had no shoulders, and layers of autumn clothing hid any shape that a waist and hips might have offered. She kept her hands and arms close to her body and managed to do whatever she needed to do with hardly any movement. But when she held her forearms beneath her bust and shook a little there was just a hint of impropriety. 'Make no mistake,' Wycherley had once said to his face in a shaving mirror, 'Rosie Ditchen is a woman with plenty held in.'

The Palfreyman wasn't a boozer. If a man wanted jostle and noise, he could go to the Station Hotel. And if he needed to fight – well, the Hoboken Arms was a rough house on Goodladies Road. The little Palfreyman was a pub for sitting in and watching. That's why Rosie Ditchen kept a chair in the corner behind the door. Sometimes strangers would come in and she would observe them, often drawing peculiar conclusions. But she was careful to keep these thoughts to herself. The Palfreyman was not a place for speaking in, Rosie thought. Oh, now and then she might exchange a word with Rough Tom who, on odd days, sat in another corner playing solitaire with dominoes (or using the little black bricks to build square looking castles on his table top). But Tom wasn't in tonight. Just Mrs Ritchers, leaning on the counter as she worked her way through the puzzle page in the morning paper, and Rosie.

And now Hubert Wycherley, the Dean's inquisitive clerk, had sat down beside her. Rosie took small mouthfuls of beer, which she chewed in a way that made her taut lips move in a circle. Quietly, without being timid, she let Hubert know that she intended to waste only a little conversation with him. She said she was all right, because she thought it reasonable that a man from the church should make such an enquiry. Then she told him that it was time he went upstairs. "They're both waiting for you. Poor little Jacobs and that horrible Berkeley."

You're an easy woman to dislike, Hubert thought. "But you will look at my calculations?" he said.

Rosie laid a hand on the satchel which he had propped against a leg of her chair. "Of course I will," she said.

When he had gone, the landlady asked, "What's it all about?" although it was none of her business.

"Shaking Jacobs says that the Dean's Clerk wants to stop the dog fighting."

6

Sixteen years later, Rosie would remember his heavy footsteps on the staircase. Loud and doom laden, with uncertain timing. "Like a church bell in a wilderness," she would say. "Tolling for a lost soul."

* * *

In the graveyard, the cathedral cat licked her lips. Puss didn't eat offal; she had stripped the vole to its skeleton but inched away from the bits of stomach that she had left on the edge of the path. The mongrel shrugged and went back to the cellar. And the rooks kept their station, like the guardians of a wicked night.

TWO

The Policeman

My name is Ned Machray. If you have read my memoirs of Billie Elizabeth 'Timberdick' Woodcock, you will know how I ended up. An overweight constable who wasn't very busy and spent much of his time on the fringes of a police force that would have preferred to do without him. This story explains how I started. I hope you will find someone to blame.

Wycherley was murdered in 1937. I had enrolled as a policeman six months before because my Uncle Fred thought that a uniform and shift work would provide me with some discipline and structure and a sense of what's important. 'If your life so far has been a shilling,' he said, 'you've been independent for six pence and wasted five pence halfpenny.' Uncle Fred did secret work for the government but, in those days, espionage was looked upon as seedy and regrettable and a family, like ours, that counted on good manners and sportsmanship kept quiet about a spy in their family tree. My uncle had no children and he may have had me in mind as his successor. That's what some people thought. But Fred and I never spoke of it.[1]

You were right, Uncle Fred. I was twenty-seven and should have been ready to move on from my lackadaisical years of drifting from job to job and making the most of girlfriends that I didn't really like. But I soon began to question whether walking a beat was going to give me sufficient sense of purpose. I had an indulgent ritual of asking myself, over each evening cocoa, what I had added to the world since getting up that morning (I got low marks for too long before I

---

1 I dabbled during the Second World War but, although my work was eventually brought to Churchill's notice, I knew that I wasn't cut out for it. Curiously, spying requires a depth of loyalty that simply isn't in me.

realised that something was wrong with the question). I didn't much like policemen, that was part of the trouble, and I was too easily irritated by the way they did things. But, mainly, the problem was Ned Machray. I hadn't properly grown out of my waster's phase. I had gained an interest in dance music (from a sitting down point of view) that would grow further during the coming war. Also, I was developing an eye for the older woman. I had yet to try my luck in that direction. But let me say at the start, my investigation of Hubert Wycherley's murder won me no credit and the interest in older women brought no end of trouble.

Bachelor bobbies should have been placed in the section house, especially during the early years of their service, but a collapsing staircase and two broken drains had closed the establishment three months before I joined. Old policemen with families had been pressed to take in young colleagues as lodgers, but that didn't work and poor Sergeant Somers had been burdened with finding digs for twenty-five displaced constables. "I don't want them with unmarried women," instructed the Chief. "Unless the women are widows or spinsters beyond childbearing age." Big Elsie's circumstances were ambiguous. Her husband had walked out on her and she had taken a lover who spent most of his time at sea. She was in her mid-forties and had the old fashioned strength of a laundry woman. She had been so keen to have a new policeman in her house that she badgered the sergeant's office until he gave in. "You'll like her, young Ned. Have you read Murder at The Vicarage? Well, big Elsie is just like that Miss Marples."

"Balderdash!" said Sergeant Martindale as he walked me up to Goodladies Junction for the first time. "There's something going on there and I mean to find it out." Sergeant Martindale was my patrol sergeant while Somers looked after process and accommodation; they didn't get on. "I'm not saying that money has changed hands or that sociable favours have been granted, but your landlady's got something over Dan Somers. I'll tell you one thing – you'll not find Elsie in any Agatha Christie. She's got no maid and no garden. She doesn't do knitting and she's having an affair with a sea captain."

Also, although I didn't mention it, she was too fond of showing off the shape of her bottom. She was always bending over to tidy up or polish or scoop or put things right. I had been in the house for less than two hours when it first happened. Elsie had been clearing the grate in her parlour when she called out with such urgency that I ran into the room. There it was, as broad as any mare's rump, stuck in the air and rocking from side to side. There had been many occasions since. I think that her predilection went as far as allowing chastely glimpses up her skirt. Especially when I was at the bottom of the staircase and she was at the top. "Now, stay there, Edward," she would say and scratch her thigh so that her dress rode up closer to the knee. "I was going to say something but, no, it's gone." There was much about Elsie that I wasn't sure of.

My night duty always found room for a stand-easy at Elsie's. I would get there by eleven and two warm muffins would be waiting on the table. Sometimes, her timing was so precise that knobs of butter would still be melting into the golden crusts as I got to her table. Elsie would have thick brown tea mashing in her little blue teapot. She always made enough for a cup each and some left over so that she could top me up when I was half way down. I hoped that she would have the wireless going and we would catch the dance band programme on the BBC. But Elsie was in charge of what was allowed and not allowed each night. It wasn't good to ask. Anyway, my view of late night radio had changed with the cancellation of 'Henry Hall's Hour' in the summer.

Our clocks were wrong on the night Wycherley died; I thought I was early but Elsie remarked, "You're a little late, this evening, dear." She watched my expression as I tasted the muffins. "They've been cooling for a few minutes," she explained.

We didn't sit together. I parked myself at the table while Elsie kept cave through the window above the kitchen sink. We thought that Sergeant Martindale would try to catch us out and, if Elsie spotted him in time, I could bolt through her front door and still make it to the top of Harold Street before him.

"You're very lucky," she said.

"I know." (She was always reminding me.) "I should be in the section house."

"You're very lucky indeed," she repeated. "Hot muffins, when you should be out walking in the cold. Why, you're not half way through your shift yet."[2]

Then silly Annie Ankers came running from the back alley shouting all kinds of alarm. She had run her fingers through her hair and she looked like a thistle after a downpour. She rapped on the window. "You! Ned in there. Murder's been done in the Palfreyman's top room!"

I jumped to my feet but I couldn't get out of the house because Annie was barging her way through the back door and Elsie was holding on to the scruff of my neck.

"You're not going anywhere without you're properly dressed," said Elsie, tucking me in and pulling my collar into shape. "Now, dear. You know what to do, don't you? Put your hands in your pockets so that you don't touch anything. Check that the body is a dead one, then close up the room and don't allow anyone in. The station will send a detective, though they'll have to get one out of bed at this time of night, so it could be an hour before he turns up. Try to remember who's in the pub and anything unusual, like furniture in odd places. Draw a picture of it all, Ned. Yes, that's a good idea. Do you want me to phone the station from here or do you want to do it from the Palfreyman?"

"You can't from here. They'll guess."

"Oh Neddie, Neddie. They know. Of course, they know. Otherwise, they wouldn't know how to catch us out. It's the rules of the game. They have to know."

I stood in the middle of the kitchen with my helmet, gloves, cape, torch and truncheon arranged about me.

"Come on." Annie danced on her feet. "I'll take you."

Elsie told her sternly, "No. You've got to get back. Your Joshua's waiting for you."

"No. I'll show Ned where it is."

"You know you mustn't do that."

"I can! I can!"

---

[2] In those days, our night duty was a twelve hour shift starting at six o'clock. We had a half hour refreshment stop at midnight or one o'clock. If our shift was extended to ten in the morning, we got two hours rest in the middle of the night without pay.

"Do as I say," Elsie barked.

Mrs Ankers blinked and bit her lip. I thought that she was ready to weep.

Elsie patted my shoulders. "Now, off you go," she said. "You'll be fine. I'll deal with Annie once you've gone."

With that, she packed me off to the Palfreyman and my first murder. I quick marched for seven minutes; the cathedral was chiming the three-quarter hour and the fox coloured mongrel watched as I hesitated at the telephone box at the corner of Harold Street. I wondered if I should summon help immediately. The 999 call had been introduced only a few months before and here was my chance to use it, but Elsie's molly-coddling made me think that it could all be a joke. I half expected to find a Guy Fawkes hanging from the Palfreyman's banister with a knife in his straw belly. After all, I had been their bobby for only a few weeks and, no doubt, I had to suffer such pranks before I could be accepted. So I carried on. The mongrel trod away to Cathedral Close and I turned left to the Palfreyman.

The Austin was standing at the pavement, the hurricane lamp hanging over its engine, but the owner was missing.

Miss Ditchen was standing on the pub's doorstep, her arms folded beneath her bust and her face tut-tutting like a disgruntled aunt. "They're all upstairs," she announced. "You'll need to take careful note of what you find." She let me pass, then called, "I'll be in the saloon if you want to speak with me. I take it you will." Mrs Ritchers and Michael the mechanic were already descending the narrow staircase. I told them all to wait with Rosie and made my way to the first floor front.

The Dean's Clerk had tried to look over his shoulder as he fell so his body ended up face down with twisted legs and a cocked head. His mouth was open in the shape of a horrible scream. I wondered if his neck was broken. Blood trickled from the corners of his mouth in a grotesque parody of a vampire, a caricature that was reinforced by his black clothes, spiky white hair and the undead stare in his eyes. I didn't see the wound to his head until I stepped over the body. The back of his skull had been broken into, as cleanly as a chisel might be driven into a tin box or a kitchen fork stuck in the flesh of a baked apple. The blood had mixed with white juice and other matters to make a mud pie – pat-a-cake, pat-a-cake – in the puddle of his exposed brain. The pie had the tang of something yellow. The blood that had trickled, then dripped, then seeped into the carpet had left a dark red patch, the shape of a naughty stain in a wet bed.

The window was open, and knocked against its frame as it swung to and fro. The light bulb swung on its long twisted cord. I backed away and felt my way along the landing, keeping my eyes closed and holding the rail. I felt sick. I couldn't stop repeating 'pat-a-cake, pat-a-cake' in my head. When I recalled the yellowy smell, the nausea got too much for me. I pulled my helmet off just in time to hold it as a bucket.

Oh God. Oh God, I've been sick with my first body.

"Have you found him, Ned?" Mrs Ritchers called from the bottom step. "He's in the front guest room."

I locked myself in the toilet and washed most of it from the inside of my hat. Then I padded it out with Bronco tissue and pressed in my leather gloves to keep the paper in place. I tried to blame Elsie's cold muffins. They were doughy and tacky, not hot and airy. If it wasn't for Elsie's baking, I would have managed Hubert Wycherley without any problem.

I came out to the landing again, the wet helmet swinging from the knuckles of my left hand. The house felt cold and empty, and the noise from the bar downstairs felt too far away. I felt faint. At one end of the passage, through the bedroom door, I could see the crown of Wycherley's open head, his broken wrist and a bloodied shirt cuff. At the other end was a tall window without a curtain at the top of the stairs. I could hear a back yard gate swinging on its hinges. It all felt eerie and unreal. I dithered on the landing for a few more minutes. The truth was, I didn't know what to do next.

"You'll want to telephone your police station," said Mrs Ritchers when I returned to the saloon.

Yes, I said. Thank you. I went behind the counter, took off my helmet and gloves, and dialled. Mrs Ritchers pulled a pint of mild, setting the glass close to the bakelite phone. Three faces watched me – Rosie Ditchen, Mike the mechanic and the Palfreyman's landlady – I could hear the phone ringing at the other end but the constable was away from the enquiry desk, allowing me time for second thoughts. "No," I said, replacing the receiver. "First, I want you to tell me what happened."

"I'll tell you what happened," the mechanic said eagerly. "He flew clean out the window and landed in Sid's coal cart." His face was smudged with clogs of dirty engine grease and exhaust soot was in his hair. He was wiping his hands on a faded orange towel, now patterned by soiled fingers.

"What have you been doing?" I asked.

"I went outside to work on my Ten-Four. Who says I shouldn't have? If you ask me, Sidney was waiting. Ready and waiting."

"Well, no-one is asking you," said Mrs Ritchers. "PC Machray, this is a quiet pub. A corner pub, if you will. Comfortable beds with fresh breakfasts and small rooms to take quiet drinks in, that's what we offer. And it's made the Palfreyman a regular choice for the small number of commercials who give me the best part of my living. Also, I encourage the local hobby groups to hold their monthly meetings upstairs. I provide quarter cut sandwiches at a fair price and the members promise to drink a pint or two in the bar before leaving. That's what was happening this evening. Hubert Wycherley wanted to meet with Berkeley and Jacobs in circumstances that wouldn't be disturbed."

"So who jumped out of the window?" I asked

"Soapy did," retorted the mechanic. "Soapy Berkeley. He didn't hesitate a second. Clean through it." He demonstrated with his greasy hands. "Clean into Sid's coal cart."

Miss Ditchen, seated in the corner, asked quietly, "Has anyone seen the goings of Shaking Jacobs?"

"I can't say as I saw him go up," Mrs Ritchers admitted.

"And what about the deanery papers?"

"He left them with you," Mrs Ritchers insisted. "You know that's what he did, Rosie Ditchen."

Miss Ditchen argued, "But you told him to put them down."

"I did not. I told him to put his hat down."

"What I'm saying is, there are no papers here now, are there? Now, look."

"Who found the body?" I asked.

14

Mrs Ritchers told the story. "Our Michael, here, came running in. 'Heavens,' he shouted. 'Heavens, you should have seen it!' And I nearly said, 'There's no-one called Evans in here, but then I heard someone shouting, 'Murder!' 'Oh God, mother,' he yells. 'Downright murder.' 'Now Rosie,' I said. 'Go to the top of Harold Street and shout for Ned. He's our copper now. He'll know what's to be done.' But she says she's not going anywhere."

"I was taking it all in," said the buttoned-up woman in the corner. "And, when I'm ready, I shall tell."

Mrs Ritchers face burned. "So I said to Michael, 'Hurry to the crossroads and shout for little Annie. Explain what's upstairs.' I said, 'Tell her to run for Elsie's young copper.' Didn't I?"

"I didn't want to," added Michael. "You can't trust Annie Ankers to do anything. She's simple. I said it'd be better if I went myself."

"But I said, no. I couldn't allow Michael to be away from the scene for more than a moment, could I? He was a witness, wasn't he? An important witness. 'Besides,' I said. 'You watch what you say about our Annie. She's no more simple than you are and she takes care over her errands.' Isn't that just what was said and how it happened?"

"Who shouted, 'Oh God mother'?" I asked.

Mrs Ritchers shook her head. Rosie said that it must have been Berkeley. But no, said the mechanic, Berkeley had already jumped from the window.

"We don't know," said Mrs Ritchers.

"And Mr Berkeley jumped out of the window?" I queried.

"Yes," said Michael.

"So what happened to Mr Jacobs?"

My witnesses looked from one to another.

"We don't know," said Mrs Ritchers.

* * *

They got a sour detective called Gutterman out of bed. He turned up with a stale taste in his mouth and his tie undone around a whiskery neck. His brown brogues had been polished for the morning, but his suit jacket and the seat of his trousers were baggy so he couldn't look smart or clean. He had an unwashed feel about him.

15

He knew how to do the job but he was determined to keep that knack to himself. He looked at the outside of the building for a long time; he stood in the middle of the road, his hands in his pockets, flexing his uncomfortable feet in his shoes and screwing up his mouth so that it creased his nose and made his eyes wince.

He came inside and studied the angle of the staircase from different positions on the ground floor. Then he went through the bar and the kitchen and seemed very satisfied when he had gained a good idea of the back yard and its possibilities. When, at last, he spoke to the witnesses in the saloon, his questions were peculiar. How often was the kitchen floor cleaned and did they always use the same mop? And did the draymen have the brewery's key to the cellar?

"OK, I think I'll get me a shave," he said. "They'll have a spare razor in one of the bedrooms. Lad, you wait outside and make sure no-one comes in."

I stood sentry for twenty minutes. The doctor arrived and I let him in. And Mrs Ankers, from the other side of the junction, came in her dressing gown to find out what was happening. But she got no closer than the opposite pavement. Then Gutterman came to the door. Drying his face and hands on a dishcloth, he said, "Make yourself scarce, boy. A superintendent's on his way and he'll bring the city's Chief Constable with him, I shouldn't wonder. Take a look around the streets, if you like. See if you can find a bloody hammer or something. But don't get caught here when the top brass turn up. It's not a good thing, lad. They don't like too much ambition."

I walked to the crossroads and stood in the porch of the corner shop. I heard a front door open in the close and I peered around the corner to see Mrs Ankers again. She held her nightclothes close to her chest and beckoned me.

Her husband pulled the chain of the outside privy and, on his way back to the kitchen, called out, "Come indoors, you old slack. You'll hear all the gossip in the morning. Soon enough."

"Elsie knows what I'm doing," she shouted back. She stooped to place a saucer of milk on the doorstep.

"Good evening again, Annie," I said. "You got back safely, I see."

"I'm not scared of Elsie. You think I am, don't you?" Then the woman pushed her head forward and asked urgently, "What's Rosie Ditchen been saying about me? What's she told you?"

"Nothing at all," I said quietly. Her husband was in the scullery now.

"She's got secrets about me and Elsie. That's what they say. Rosie Ditchen's got big secrets."

"I've hardly spoken to Miss Ditchen."

"Well, it seems to me that you ought to do a lot of speaking to her." Mrs Ankers had her hair in twists, her lips were pale and she had worry spots on her nose. "You'll want to have a look around Bert Wycherley's place," she said and produced a key from the folds of her nightclothes. "I do bits for him in the mornings. It's so wrong, you know, a man of the cloth taking his own life like that. I've said to my Josh – I don't know how many times – that man's too much on his own. It never does any good, being on your own. It gets you thinking too deeply about things." Then she leaned forward. "He's got a tasty bit of fresh bacon in his larder. He won't be needing it now, will he?"

I heard Mr Ankers shout, "Bed woman! It's the middle of the night."

"Another day and I'll tell you all about Rosie, Elsie and little Annie," she said, handing me the key. "We were together at school." With a comic hint of a curtsey, she dipped back into her hallway but held the door open a couple of inches as she said, "If Rosie's made a mistake, give her a chance to put things right. She's always doing it. Making mistakes then finding ways to make up for them."

I tucked the key in my pocket and continued my walk down the close. Behind me, Mr Ankers was shouting impatiently and the wooden door closed.

My footsteps echoed against the stone facings of the terraced cottages and the churchyard wall. Curtains twitched at Number 17 and I heard a staircase creak, two doors up, as someone sat on the bottom step. Folk were listening to my progress along their narrow pavement and, when my footsteps ceased, they would know that I had turned into the jitty for a smoke.

I had been practising my policeman's walk so I was pleased with the sound my footsteps made. A good bobby feigns busy activity in each stride but travels not very far at all. The knack is to let your foot veer to the side, then return to the ground only a few inches from where it started. But you mustn't let the movement become a comic dance, so it needs to be completed subtly. Sergeant Martindale – who had coached me in this matter – said that a policeman proceeds in a careful dawdle and I think that's a pretty good description.

Standing at ease, beneath the brick archway of Pardoner's Lane which was no more than a covered footpath, presented an opportunity to rehearse that copper's movement of lifting himself on the balls of his feet. Generally, the fingers should be interlocked behind the back and a good exchange of breath allows the officer to exhale a knowing 'hmmm' or 'I see' as if passers-by are witnessing the process of detective deduction. But my arms weren't long enough – or my waist was too large – so I laid my hands across the front of my tunic. Of course, this accentuated my belly and even suggested an attitude of prayer. I expected the scallywags to nickname me 'the vicar' before long.

I fished my pipe from my breast pocket and charged it from a pouch of fresh tobacco. Rennie Teggs, the tobacconist on the corner of Goodladies Road, had settled in the neighbourhood only a few weeks before me. He was sure that an immigrant family should be friends with the local beat officer. 'I make no bones about this,' he told me. He had presented me with my first pipe and recommended a special Russian mixture of black tobacco. 'It's rich but leaves no dottle in the bowl,' he promised. We laughed at my early attempts to manage the pipe. 'No, no, my good friend. A gentleman never fights with his pipe. You must coax it. A man of good manners regards his pipe as a countryman treats his favourite hound. The dog may be naughty, a renegade, but the master must never bully. You must treat your pipe this way; together, you have many pleasant hours in store.'

Sheltered by the porch of Pardoner's Lane, I got the thing going with just four matches. Two trawler men, in oilskins and boots with bits of fish stuck on them, emerged from one of the crooked lanes. They didn't notice me and their talk of card games and bookies' runners carried on from one end of the close to the other. As they reached the crossroads, a Standard motorcar drew up and the Chief Constable emerged from the back seat. He dismissed the driver, then stood in the middle of the junction and looked around.

I put my palm over the red glow of the pipe and took a step back into the alley. The Chief Constable was a small man with a shape and stature that made me think of an undernourished childhood. His head was narrow and his eyes seemed to slope down at the sides. His nose was bent and, like his mouth and chin, looked as if it had been pushed forward. He disguised this awkwardness with a full but well-barbered beard. He stepped towards the cobbled roadway of the close and I had an uneasy feeling that he was looking for me. He already had me marked as an indolent bobby and he would be ready to give a poor assessment of my work that night. His prejudice was only a little unfair, I have to say. I had spent the first two weeks in the force helping in the Chief's garden. His wife had duly reported on my prospects and then passed me to the Deputy's wife. She had me shopping and moving wardrobes for another week and, although she talked much about tea, I never saw a cup. The upshot of all this induction was a general nervousness that probationer Machray was not going to make the grade. I was sure that if the Chief had been told that I had found Wycherley's body, he'd want to know if I had fouled up the investigation from the start.

Gutterman must have posted a look-out, for the Chief had been at the crossroads for only a few seconds before the clever-dick detective came up from the Palfreyman. The two men shook hands; neither of them wore a uniform so they couldn't properly salute. Then the Chief tucked his ebony walking stick under one arm and they went off together.

I stepped forward and got the pipe going again. I saw that the cathedral cat had stepped up to her place on Mrs Ankers' doorstep; she drank from the saucer of milk with a smugness that was close to cockiness. (Cockiness? It was this downright arrogance that made the other creatures want to see her brought down.) I noticed that the mongrel was curious about something in the long grass of the graveyard. He had his nose down and his hind legs were steering him round in a circle. I observed for several minutes – puffing on my pipe, lifting it from my mouth when the temptation to chew the stem got too much – and I realised that he had found a hedgehog. The dog was too wise to tamper with the ball of spines but he wanted to aggravate.

My footsteps echoed through the close again. I climbed the three

19

steps to Wycherley's door and let myself into his house. The hall was cramped; I had to step to one side to avoid the steep staircase and, immediately to the left, three further steps took me into the sitting-room and, beyond that, the kitchen. Somehow, the kitchen became the first floor at the back of the house. It looked out onto a veranda and then an untidy garden. I could see the grey shapes of things dumped outside.

I stood my smelly helmet on the beech draining board and draped my cloak and tunic over the backs of two chairs. I noticed three speckled brown eggs, uncracked on a plate, with rashers of bacon in grease-proof paper and an empty half pint tankard. I found a jar of Jeyes under the sink and went to work with a scouring pad on the inside of my hat. Then I rubbed it out with a damp cloth and, drying my hands on a tea towel, walked through to the sitting-room.

Of course, it was nonsense to think that I could learn a dead man's character by looking at the chairs he had sat in. But it was very easy to picture the Dean's Clerk resting in the high-backed armchair, his feet in carpet slippers tipped over the brass lip of the hearth, his left hand inclining – almost furtively – to the little glass of whiskey on the occasional table, and his eyes reading this week's library book through rimless spectacles on the end of his nose. Wycherley was dead but the cut glass tumbler, polished and sparkling, was waiting on the table. The spectacle case was on the mantelpiece. And the novel from the circulating library had been balanced on a wicker basket of chopped sticks. The fire had gone out but the spent coals were still hot and, when I leaned forward to pick up the book, I noticed a baked potato at the edge of the grate. That gave me a different idea. I plucked it from the coals and, bouncing it from palm to palm because it was so hot, took it through to the kitchen. I dug a sturdy frying pan from a cupboard, causing a great clatter of falling saucepans, and got a knob of fat going on the stove. I fried the bacon, singing lightly to myself as I always did when I cooked, then cracked the three speckled eggs into the dripping. While it all popped, crackled and spat in the pan, I cut two thick slices from a handy loaf and spread them, generously, with marge from the cold slab in the larder. Then I sat down at the table. I burst the potato skin and poured egg yolk over the insides. I paused before tucking in, but only to relish the prospect of this midnight feast. "Far better than Elsie's muffins," I said aloud, but I needed a little more room to make the most of it so I took off my tie, slipped the collar stud free and loosened the top three buttons of my flies. The dead man had known the true comforts of a bachelor's life, I reflected.

Twenty minutes later, I was perched on a windowsill at the front of the house overlooking the empty close. I had a mug of his Mackeson in one hand and his library book in the other. I kept closing the book so that I could bring some fingers to my mouth; the fry-up was repeating. But I felt extraordinarily relaxed and I saw how Wycherley would have sat here at night, reading by the streetlamp and looking out over the dark shapes of the almshouses and the graveyard. The heavy curtains had the design and texture of something that had been taken down from a church. When I disturbed them, hoping for more light, I noticed a spent cocktail glass on the ledge. The odour of gin came up from the white creamy residue; the drink had been taken that evening but Wycherley wasn't the cocktail type. He had welcomed a visitor into his home and they had stood at this window as they talked, just hours before he died.

I also recognised a less charming aspect of Wych's personality. He had pencilled on the title page of The Riddle of the Sands, 'Every man his own secret agent'. I thought, what sort of chap thinks that a subsequent reader would value his pompous comments? But then I realised that the little stage had been carefully managed. The supper ready for cooking. The waiting chair at the fireside. The spectacles and whisky glass waiting to be used. And the book? What if Wycherley had known that The Riddle of The Sands, with his handwritten annotation, would never be passed to a subsequent reader? Had he left it behind as a clue – 'Every man his own secret agent' – because the Dean's Clerk expected to be murdered that night?

I decided to browse around for other clues. I climbed the steep staircase to the study. There, I found the evidence of his work. Road maps and coastal charts and page upon page of sketches. I was new to the area but I was sure that he had been recording the topography of some headlands, about twenty miles from the city. "Every man his own secret agent," I said aloud. "And a riddle of the sands. Our sands. Sands close to home."

When I emerged from the dead man's house, the close was brightening up to a grey dawn but still deserted; if anything, it seemed more deserted now than at any time during the night. The animals no longer prowled the churchyard and folk who had been happy to sit up and watch at midnight now clung to the bedclothes for a few extra minutes. And the policemen had withdrawn, every one of them. There was no sentry at the Palfreyman's door, no patrol vehicles near the crossroads and no-one was looking for me.

I proceeded steadily down the close, across the junction and towards the top of Harold Street. I was supposed to phone the police station at twenty past and ten minutes to every hour. Working with CID gave me an excuse for missing most of these 'points' but, now that I was less than an hour from booking off, I thought it would be good form to phone in.

"Go home, Machray," said the station officer. (There was hardly room for me in the telephone box, with my cape and helmet, gloves and torch, heavy boots, a ready pen and pocket book and the packet of papers from Wycherley's study.[3]) "We've written you off to the detectives. It's here in the log. 'Twelve o'clock, PC Machray to investigations.' Go home, and we'll see you tonight. Parade at fifteen minutes to six."

---

3 It could have been worse. The Chief Constable had recently announced that 'because of the deteriorating situation' binoculars would be issued to each constable. There was never enough to go round so priority was given to those beats with a view of the shore. In 1941 it was decided that only policemen on bicycles would carry them, because someone had remarked that a walking policeman could easily be grabbed and strangled by his binocular strap. But the equipment was too useful not to go missing. At the end of the war it was decided that deficiencies would not be made up.

THREE

My Sergeant and the Landlady

"Good Lord, you look worn out."

Big Elsie opened the door in a house dress, a paisley patterned pinnie and a pair of stretched and floppy slippers. Three neat curling clips –with tissue and elastic – pinned the hair on each side of her head, just above the ears.

"I can tell you what happened, Elsie." She had mothered me so carefully before packing me off to the Palfreyman that I was as eager to tell her what I had found as I would have been to boast to my own proud parent.

"Oh no, no, no. All that can wait. Young Ned, you're out on your feet. Why don't you go upstairs and nap beneath the blankets for a couple of hours. Get these clothes off – they must weigh a ton – and brush the dust from your hair. (You've got egg down your front, you know.) No, no ifs or buts, get yourself up there. I'll bring you some Bournvita when you've settled. Don't worry, I always knock first."

I did as I was told. I discarded the damp helmet and my cloak at the bottom of the stairs and went up to the bedroom. I stripped off, dropping the uniform to the floor rather than the convenient bedside chair, then disappeared under the blankets (she had taken the sheets off my bed for washing). I closed my eyes but had no intention of going to sleep before Elsie came in the room. My head was full of too much. My first dead body. My smart questioning of witnesses. And the clue of the white creamy cocktail.

I was alone for only a few minutes. Elsie grumbled and tut-tutted as she went around the carpet, picking up my mess. Whenever she bent down, I fancied once again that she was deliberately showing me how big her bottom was or inviting me to peep, just a little, up her dress. Then she came close, her bosoms big in their brassiere beneath her dress, and tucked the blankets under my mattress. "Now, what are you doing in there?" she asked. "Nothing naughty, I hope." And she emitted a long low 'hmm' suggesting that it would be better if she didn't enquire further.

"I've got so much to tell you," I said like a child, home from an exciting day at school.

Then we were interrupted by a loud knocking on the front door. Elsie peered through the curtains and announced, "Gerald Martindale."

"Crike, no."

"We'd better not ignore the good sergeant," she said and stepped towards the bedroom door.

"Wait," I said urgently.

"I certainly won't," she said. "You can get dressed in your own company, Ned Machray. I came up here to tell you that Shaking Jacobs is in the kitchen and wanting to see you. And, Mr Machray, I'll have you know that I came up for no other reason."

Sergeant Martindale was waiting at the bottom of the stairs. He had taken off his helmet to be polite and he was holding it beneath one arm in the way that officers pose for studio photographs.

"I thought I would find you here. Have you finished your shift early?"

I dithered on the third step of the staircase. "The station officer said."

"And where have you been since one in the morning? Arnie Gutterman says you disappeared. The Chief was looking for you, you know." He was a gruff man, immensely strong and so much a policeman that the chin strap of his helmet had permanently creased his silver side whiskers. Always, his voice, his stare and sometimes merely the sound of his footsteps made me want to fidget in my boots. I couldn't picture anyone telling my sergeant what to do.[4]

---

4 All this was through the eyes of an immature twenty-seven year old. In 1940, when others had gone off to war, Gerald Martindale was promoted to inspector. It was a responsibility that he couldn't manage and he was publicly berated by a middle ranking Home Guard commander.

"Mr Gutterman said I was to look around," I pleaded lamely.

"You didn't call in," he persisted. "You missed all your points." I tried to think quickly. "I'd been written off." I repeated, "The station officer said."

He decided that good manners prevented him from pursuing the matter in front of my landlady. "Elsie, will you make us a pot of your famous tea?" he asked. "As thick as nut soup." Without a word – but with a cold face that scorned Martindale for pushing his luck – Elsie retired to the kitchen and I suggested that we should sit in the front room. "Yes, invite me into your parlour, sonny." He considered the state of me, then tapped my chest. "A fool would suppose that you were more at home here than you should be."

"Serge, I should explain."

He raised a hand. "PC Machray, please don't think that you are the first constable to have his conkers cosseted under this roof." He took the comfortable armchair and told me to sit at the other side of the hearth. Elsie's front room clock and a picture of her estranged husband were on the mantelpiece between us but Sergeant Martindale and I were still close enough to knock knees. "The boys say she keeps a picture of the Navy C-in-C at her bedside. Her husband in the parlour. Her sailor by her bed. That's what they say."

I said quietly, "I don't think the boys know anything about what's at her bedside."

He took an empty pipe from his pocket and smacked it against the heel of his left hand. "Worst place for clocks," he remarked. "The smoke from the fire clogs their lungs."

"She hardly uses the room," I said. "She lives in the scullery."

Martindale thought twice, then he put the pipe away. Elsie was making plenty of noise at the draining board. We all knew that she could hear every word we said.

"A Scotland Yard detective has been given the case. It may be that he will want a few words with you. A few words, Constable. Make sure that's all he gets. Don't imagine that he wants to know what you think, because he doesn't. And if he does, it's not your place to tell him. If necessary, I'll tell him what you think. We all know that Arnold Gutterman's more than capable of reporting what happened at the Palfreyman last night." He added, "We like sound coppers, round here, not bright penny peelers. See yourself as one of Morrison's Light Horse, do you?"

"Not at all, Sergeant," I said smartly.

"Got a famous uncle, have you?"

"I've never mentioned my uncle," I replied curtly.

"I could take half your week's pay because of your conduct tonight. But I won't. Instead, you and I will agree that, as soon as this job's done, you'll put yourself up for a move to another constabulary. We won't want you back in this division. Meantime, count every rule that you break because if you dilly-dally for longer than I like, I will charge you with every one of your transgressions."

"Where do I report, Serge?"

"Report, Serge?"

"For the Scotland Yard man. When he wants to see me."

"At the station, of course. Tonight, fifteen minutes before duty time."

Then, on the doorstep, he softened a little. "I'm giving you good advice, lad, and I don't care who's listening. Don't get too close to the public you serve. You're 'a part of' or 'apart from'. Some chaps try to be both or swap from one to the other. But they can't. Don't get too close and don't try to give more that you can deliver. Give your people a good coppersworth – they shouldn't expect more."

* * *

Although Jacobs was sitting with a beaker of hot tea at the kitchen table, he still had his coat and scarf on. He started to lift himself from the chair as I walked in, but Elsie stopped him. She was sitting next to him and, because she kept her legs to one side instead of under the table, she looked especially close to him. She watched him like a mother hen.

"I wasn't there, Mr Mac."

"He doesn't like to be called Mac," she said quietly. "Call him, Mr Ned."

"The folk in the Palfreyman said I should speak with PC Machray so that's why I've come here."

"Mr Ned. Not PC Machray. Mr Ned, because he's one of us. He's our copper. Aren't you, Ned?"

I stepped forward. "Really, it doesn't matter what you call me."

"Well I wasn't there," he insisted. "I was supposed to be. Wychers had called a meeting and I said I'd be there – but when I was home, waiting for nine o'clock, I thought, 'Don't have anything to do with this, Jacobs. Stay out of it.' So I told my wife that I wasn't going out after all. I said, the world is full of terrible warnings and we must tread carefully. Every one of us. Oh, God, those poor people. I knew that I was right. I sat with the wireless until half past nine. Then I went up."

Elsie stood beside him. She put a hand on his shoulder and his worried head leaned thankfully into the warmth of her motherly bust. "There's so much of it, Els. And just look what happened. I listened to the warnings in my head and I was right. Hubert's dead."

"The poor people?" I queried but Elsie put a fingertip to her lips.

"Shaky's been very saddened by the airship that burned in America. But we've listened to you, haven't we, Shaky, and we know that we mustn't fret over things that we can't change."

"Like the bombs in Spain," Jacobs emphasised. "That's what Hubert said. He said it would happen here if we didn't do something. He had plans, you see, Mr Machray."

I asked, "What was the meeting about?"

He looked at Elsie and, when she nodded, he explained, "Mr Wycherley wanted someone to help him. It had to be an ordinary bloke who could do things without people remarking. It would be all right for people to see him but they should always think that he couldn't be doing anything important. That's why he came to me. But I said he shouldn't rely on me. I said that'd be a bad idea. And I told him to ask Soapy and Soapy said that we both could do it. I said, we're only doing it because it's you who's asking, Mr Wycherley. And he said that was very good."

"Why would you do it for Mr Wycherley but no-one else?"

"Because he wasn't a man who'd waste his time. He was quiet, wasn't he, Els? He was either indoors or cycling on his own. Often, you'd see his light on late; he was always working on something."

"Or reading at his landing window," I said.

"How do you know that, Mr Machray? I mean, Constable Machray."

"I don't really. I was showing off and you've just taught me a lesson."

He didn't understand.

"I should listen to people and not be smart."

"Anyway, Mr Wycherley wanted us to walk along one of the coast roads at night and observe."

I nodded. "He'd found a weakness in our air defence and wanted to prove it."

"What makes you say that?"

"He had made notes on some charts. Just workings-out, really. I think he was going to present Soapy Berkeley and you with the final version last night. We know that Wycherley was meant to bring some papers to the Palfreyman. Rosie says she saw them in his music satchel but no-one knows where they are now. I've looked around his home and there are other papers, sketches of the headlands. That's all I know."

"Well, Soapy says it's more likely to be about dogs. Mr Wycherley loved our cats and dogs. But I wouldn't know anything about that, would I? Because I didn't go to the Palfreyman."

I walked across the kitchen, unlocked the back door and stood on the step, watching the grey sky as it moved above us. Somewhere, an old Lysander was trying to land but raised its engine and went around again.

"You don't believe me," he said, still at the table.

"Where did he want you to patrol?"

"I don't know. That's what he was going to tell us, but I stayed at home."

"Now you shut that door, young Ned," said Elsie. "You're just out of bed and you'll catch your death."

When I took a couple of steps down the alley at the back of Elsie's house, Jacobs ran to the door. "Do you believe me?" he called. "Do you believe I wasn't there?"

"Of course, Ned does." Elsie had her hands on his shoulders, encouraging him back into the kitchen. "And, Ned, I'll not tell you again. Come in here with us."

28

When Jacobs had left, and Elsie and I were alone in her front parlour, she said, "Your sergeant had no right to say what he did, no right at all." She was dusting away his presence. Straightening cushions. Adjusting ornaments. "No policeman can say he's been comforted beneath my roof. 'Cosseted conkers', I'll be damned before any such thing goes on here." She told me to get out of her armchair. "You know we don't sit in here. Not in the front room."

I said, before moving, "I met Annie Ankers again last night. In the close. If Rosie's made a mistake, she said, I should give her a chance to put things right. Annie said that Rosie's always doing it. 'Making mistakes then finding ways to make up for them.' What do you think, Elsie?"

"Oh yes," she said, smiling at the thought. "If Rosie did a murder, it would be for the sake of justice. Me? I'd do a murder because I'm a bully."

"And Annie?"

"I can't think why she would. She's not got it in her. But she would have to confess. She couldn't deny it afterwards."

I got up from the chair.

"But Ned," she said, making me turn around when I reached the door. "None of us did it."

FOUR

The House on the Shore

Before the early morning ferry was properly tied up, the deck hand slipped the chain and a score of cyclists spilled onto the jetty. Most walked with their bikes, others scooted awkwardly and some were already on their saddles and pushing hard up the slope. I let them hurry on. My work shift didn't start until six in the evening so I had all day to search for the scene in Wycherley's watercolour.

By the time I got free of the town, the paperboys had emptied their sacks, the grocers were stacking their displays of vegetables on the pavements and school caretakers had unlocked the playground gates. I left all that behind.

I cycled as close to the shore as the paths would allow. A light railway ran along that stretch of coast; its top speed was little more than a brisk marching pace so something of a race developed between us. I would gain ground each time the engine driver was delayed at a halt – these put-me-downs were twelve feet of wooden platform with little or no shelter from the weather; they were one up from bus stops – then I would hear the tiny engine gather speed and it would overhaul me, but never by so much that I couldn't hope to catch up next time. In the end, I was beaten by the long run in to the fisherman's pier at a little seaside village. The engineer was out of his cab and waving at me when I got there. "You'd always run out of puff before me," he joked.

The line went no further. I dismounted, for I was too plump to be a natural cyclist even in those days, and walked to the edge of the grassy cliff. It was a lovely morning; fingers of flat clouds decorated an untroubled ten o'clock sky and the call of seabirds sparked overhead. The air was well washed and there was more room to breathe it, out here, away from the city. Three hundred yards to my right, a team of ratings was working to manhandle a fragile seaplane from the water's edge. The craft looked no stronger than a child's model of bamboo, balsa and rice paper. The Petty Officer was at his wit's end. He had shouted himself hoarse; he was up to his knees in seawater and he worked his arms like the sails of a windmill, but he couldn't make his raw recruits see common sense. It all looked ready to end in disaster. Two anglers on the pier were laughing at them. I wheeled my bike closer, but when I sensed that His Majesty's Fleet Air Arm thought that it might be offering too much amusement, I diverted my interest. I brought out the district Red Guide and flicked through the pages. People came to this village to turn their backs on it, wrote the editor. I caught his meaning immediately. From here, the splendid views of the busy sea lanes were so attractive that I gave no attention to the settlement that had grown behind the shore line. I left my bicycle on the bank and let myself slip down to the stony beach. A rich man's motor boat, the working boats of local fishermen, a freighter and ferry boats; all these ships shared the choppy passageways with one of the grey old cruisers of the home fleet. I hoped that I would see one of the tall ships – the Amerigo Vespucci with the tarnished livery, perhaps, or the older Sorlandet. Then, I lifted my head in time to see an early Dutch Widgeon flying in close to the shore. She turned on the wing and braked in her ungainly manner as she stuttered onto the water. Then she was gone and, although I waited for her to come again to the surface, I had to concede that her energy outstripped my patience.

Something else was happening. The majestic shape of the best liner in the world had appeared on the edge of the picture. She was miles away and looked no larger than a toy. At first, I wasn't sure that she was moving and I fixed my eyes on her, mesmerized almost, until I saw that she was putting distance between her and landmarks behind her. The Queen Mary. Her three red funnels and her bold superstructure gleamed cleanly in the sunlight. She was a bright-as-steel statement of our artistic vision, engineering skill and downright hard work. This was what set us apart from other nations on the earth: we could make this. I was immensely proud. I wanted to run along the beach, waving, although she was too far off to see me. If we can build such ships as this, I thought, no country will want to go to war against us.

She was just three years old and her presence on the horizon had drawn a modest cluster of spectators on the cliff top. I didn't want to be part of them, so I climbed back into the saddle and cycled on. Soon the houses and their people were behind me and I was in real countryside. I considered resting in a ditch and breaking open one of the beer bottles that Elsie had packed in the saddlebag, but I reminded myself that this phoney holiday had a purpose so I kept on going, down Monkey Hill and along the gorse shore. I reached the stretch of low lying headlands, broken by inlets and creeks that were no more than streams. Now I felt that I was getting somewhere and worked the pedals with renewed vigour.

The narrow broken-up lane provided a perilous cycle ride; its path bossed by the rugged coastline – one moment the road would turn back on itself, then it would lop at a camber where the softer ground had subsided and a man had to struggle to keep his handlebars straight, then there would be a steep climb, not more than twenty yards but so tall that it was all but impossible to keep pedalling.

I reached an exposed knoll where the vegetation had cleared, allowing a good view of the seashore for five miles each way, and laid the bicycle down, got out my picnic and established a nice seat on the ground. This was a bright day but I hadn't realised how sharp the wind was, the sort of chilly breeze that makes your neck ache later on. I knocked the tops off the bottles of stout, unwrapped the thick cheese cobs and tucked in.

About fifty yards along the beach, a mother, wrapped in a cheap overcoat, was sitting on a travel rug. Bags and spare sweaters were propped against her body to keep her warm. She knitted, pausing every now and then to sort out the string of wool that, for some reason, she kept wound around a bottle of pop. Her daughter played ball on the shingle. They had the place to themselves for it was too cold to sit and do nothing and, anyway, this was a poor stretch of beach; the shingle was shallow and tufts of coarse grass had broken to the surface. "Billie, watch your knees," the mother called. "You fall and cut them, you'll have scabs for weeks."

The seven-year-old saw me but wanted to
presence. She made sure that each toss of the ba
to my little camp until, with one throw that w
applause on any cricket field, the ball disappeared i
thorns to my left.

"We're waiting for Uncle Harry," she explained w   -p
to me. "He's coming down to see us today and we ca   ͜ back to
Mrs Lyons until three," This message delivered, she recovered her
ball without difficulty and hurried back to her mother.

"Here, Billie. Put your cardie on. It's lighter for you."

After lunch, I stretched out on the ground and closed my eyes for
twenty minutes while my stomach tried to settle the pickled onions
and cold eels, a mix that always plays me up.

Another twelve months and those ratings on the shore could be
fighting an enemy. Once again, I was wanting to do something. In
fact, 'doing something' got more overdue every time I thought about
it. But it was difficult to decide what to do. I told myself that it was
too early to join up. A fellow needs to see how the ground lies.
'Doing stuff' could so easily be a waste of time when my life still
lacked any real direction. Gavin Tullett, who had taught me to drive
lorries in 1932, had insisted that doing nothing wasn't at all a waste of
time. "It's waiting," he always said. "And waiting can only be wise.
Never forget that."

There was going to be a war, I was sure of that, and I was
determined that fighting for England should emerge as my destiny.
But, heavens above, I couldn't see myself as a soldier. No, I'd do
better if I followed Hubert Wycherley's lead. Every man his own
secret agent.

"Of sorts," I whispered involuntarily, my eyes still closed. "Not
like Uncle Fred, oh no. But a spy of sorts."

This idea had occurred to me when I was snooping around
Wycherley's cottage. I wasn't supposed to do that. No-one had asked
me to collect evidence. And I had decided to keep the evidence to
myself. "Just the sort of thing that spies do," I said and, without
moving the rest of my body, I managed to push my shoes and socks
off. With my eyes still closed, I found a pebble and kicked it. I was
still lying down. "And I enjoy it!"

...aking back to Elsie's place for tea and muffins on nights – ...was acting like a secret agent. But Uncle Fred was an ...comfortable niggle. I didn't want to follow Uncle Fred, (heavens, hadn't I had enough of him?) and he's been a spy.

"Of sorts," I whispered again. "A spy of sort."

A clear young voice said, "You're too fat to be a spy."

I opened my eyes and saw the girl looking down on me. I didn't say anything. My eyes winced in the bright daylight; she turned and ran away and I heard her laugh when she reached the shingle. I closed my eyes again and heard the mother and child talking and gathering things together as I drifted off to sleep.

By two o'clock the sun was getting the better of the cloudy sky and Billie and her mother had left the beach. I had napped for longer than I meant to and I knew that I needed to be starting back. But I wanted to make something of Wycherley's evidence; that was what I had come for, so I fetched the artist's book from the saddle bag and leafed through the crayoned pages.

I realised that he had tried a simple deception by drawing a mirror image of what he had seen. Twisting my neck as I looked over my shoulder and then back to the sketch pad had, I think, made it easy for me to spot this little trick.

Ten minutes later, I found what I was looking for. The house was set back from the cliff road and protected by a display of imported trees and tall hedges. But there was no mistaking it. In his drawing, Wycherley had caught the texture of the white walls and orange terracotta tiles. I knew that this was the house he had been observing. But why?

Keeping in the cover of the gorse and wild shrubs, I scampered three times along the front of the property. But I knew that I could watch for hours and nothing would happen. To do any good, I had to work with more purpose.

I jumped into an overgrown ditch and hid there while I made up my mind. Having identified Wycherley's scenery, the next step should be exploration, but trespassing was more than I had set out to do. I tried to think of an excuse that might be believed. Then I noticed the young girl playing in the ditch on the opposite side of the road. I decided that if the owners of the big house caught me

34

snooping, I could say that I was searching for a lost child. Hopefully, the infant would turn up and verify my story.

Breaking the bounds was easy enough because much of the perimeter was out of sight from the house and the hedges at the back had been recently thinned. I crossed the weeded tennis court, skirted the terrace of ornamental fishponds and found myself crouching beneath the line of the kitchen windows. The lady was calling through to an older gentleman in the conservatory. I couldn't see her at first, but the conversation told me that the man was sticking pictures into a scrapbook and she was losing patience with him. Crouching, I scurried along the veranda until the conservatory came into view.

He was a retired Admiral of sorts, as bald as a billiard ball, who mediated between our police force and port defence authorities. They called him The Commodore, but I'm sure that he hadn't been to sea for some years. During my week in the Chief Constable's house, I had taken a telephone call; the Commodore wanted to speak with the Chief's wife. I said that she wasn't in and neither was her husband. He mumbled under his breath and put the phone down; I guessed that he had little time for the Chief's wife's husband. A week later, I saw him in the corridors of our headquarters. Unlike Wycherley, who was a good draughtsman but no more, the Commodore had imaginative flair for illustration and he was presenting two sketches of our Chief Constable in his army days. Someone said that they should be hung in the foyer. No-one groaned, but the Commodore saw me wanting to. He readily identified me as the rookie on the phone and made a point of shaking my hand and calling me Edward. I didn't like him.

This time, I was careful that he didn't see me. I crawled back along the sanded flagstones and sat beneath the kitchen window. The lady had her back to me; she was preparing a tea tray but she was ready to go riding. She was well kept and confident and she called to the Commodore with a haughtiness of a lady who could hold her own. She was about my age, so he was more than thirty years her senior (not that she would have recognised any authority in that). I was sure that she was too occupied to turn around, so I took a good look at her. Tight fitting jodhpurs, brown leather boots and a horsewoman's jacket left open at the front made the most of her figure. Her black hair was drawn back from her face and wrapped into a low bun at the back of her neck. The riding helmet sat on the kitchen table but the crop hung from her hip and bounced when she moved. This lady had no intention of mixing with horses that morning. She hadn't prepared herself to get dirty or work up a sweat. Her make up was too elaborate for that – too expressive, I thought. And her manicured hands with long, varnished nails were meant to carry the leather gloves rather than test them against a set of taut reins. No, I didn't think that she had ever sat in that sort of saddle.

When I tried for a better look, she lifted the tray, turned around and raised her eyes from the doilies and cherry sticks. For a moment, I was sure that she had seen me.

"The Brigadier is waiting for me!" she was shouting.

Chair legs scraped the conservatory floor. I ducked down, stumbled and caught my ankle on the edge of the stone border of the veranda. I could hear that they were both moving to a hallway at the front of the ground floor so I scuttled around the back, passing the conservatory where the scrapbook was still open on a wrought iron table. Now I was on the opposite side of the gardens, away from the tennis courts and fishponds, and the overgrown shrubbery and hedges provided better cover. I remembered how carefully the rest of the gardens had been kept and wondered if this corner had been left deliberately rough. At one stage, I was completely hidden by twigs and greenery and found my way along a muddy path only by following the single tyre track of an old wheelbarrow. I heard an upstairs window open at the back of the house and the lady laughed excitedly. God alone knew what went on in that house! But I didn't dare look for her again. I had already recognised her in that second when she turned and looked out of the kitchen window. She was the Chief Constable's wife.

I got away through a wicket gate that put me on the edge of a deep pit. Some sort of quarry, I thought at first, but there was no sign of any industry. It was like a miniature amphitheatre with steeps sides, rutted and creviced and shored up with old beams. It was so badly drained that the walls looked ready to fall down and the floor was a mud bath. I was, perhaps, two hundred yards from the house but I could have been a world away. There was no sound of the sea and the coast road was obscured by wild trees and brambles. This was an ideal hideaway.

"It's for dog fighting."

I looked more carefully and saw seven year old Billie, buttoned up and belted in her gabardine, standing halfway down the slope.

"It's the same as one of my uncles told me of," she continued. Then, curiously, she sought to correct herself. "Told me 'have', I mean."

I smiled. "He told you of it, Billie."

"He did. Near his Harborough home, he said, and that's miles away."

Indeed, it was.

"So many miles," she said. "It would take a grown man a year to walk."

"Indeed," I conceded. "But I think this is about bonfires and beacons, Billie. Signals. Billie, do you think we have smugglers?"

Her eyes sat up in their beds. "Smugglers! Do you really think so?"

FIVE

The Man Rosie Ditchen Didn't Want

Turncott was fed up with riding in the back of the Police Wolseley. He wasn't a man who could read while travelling in a car and the soft South Downs didn't interest him. He felt disgruntled. The interview with the Commissioner had not gone well. He had been instructed to abandon a desk of unresolved files. He was to go down to the coast immediately. And then, at ten past midnight, he had learned that Sergeant Willis would be his driver. Turncott did not like policemen of Reginald Willis's ilk. They filled their heads with revolutionary ideas while resisting any new initiatives promoted by their superiors. They were either surly – which could always be dealt with – or they were clever, which could not. Furthermore, Turncott did not trust policemen who sat in cars. They had too much time to think and how could they develop a well adjusted view of the world when they probably preferred engines to people?

Sergeant Willis had suggested that they should break at the Kingfisher Inn, twenty miles back, but Turncott had ordered him to drive on. "I don't need to stretch my legs," he said.

Well, Reginald Willis very much had a need. Without seeking permission, he parked on the ridge of the high chalk hill and disappeared into the scrub. When he came back, Turncott was out of the car and leaning against the boot as he compared his map with the city that was laid out before him. "I can't work out where I'm going," he confessed, then told himself off for showing a sergeant that he was impatient. "A long winding ribbon from St Mary's Church to East Police Station, so I should be able to spot it."

"You want me to drop you in the centre, sir?"

38

"What's the talk in Peckham Garage, Sergeant?" Turncott asked, knowing that the driver would not hold back.

"The word is you only accepted the job after the Commissioner guaranteed that you'd be free of local commanders."

"You think I can barter with the Commissioner?" the detective grumbled. He had meant the remark to sound like an admonishment – but he merely sounded bitter. "You think I can draw promises from the Commissioner?"

"Just as I said, sir. I said, if the locals have been warned off, it's because they've got tacky fingers. Either that, or it's Admiralty business. The dockyard and all. Everyone knows that the Admiralty and the War Office always prefer to deal with Scotland Yard. Local Chief's aren't tame." He added 'sir' and got back in the car. "The other story is about the beat bobby. Do you know he's Fred Machray's nephew? Fred persuaded him to join the force."

"The time will come when people will call us a service, Willis. Not a force. We'll support neighbourhoods rather than enforce the rules."

"That's just fancy speaking, sir. It'd be a mess. Like this new 'Ring-For-A-Copper-Whenever-You-Need-One."

"You mean the 999 call?" Turncott allowed himself a smile; he'd not met a bobby on the beat who thought the idea was a good one.

"Don't tell me that it works," said Willis. "We'll have coppers chasing every stray dog and child's trike. I tell you, they'll give it up in twelve months."

"Come on, Sergeant, start the engine. I thought you were all for new thinking."

"We live in a world where people are growing further apart, not closer. H.G. says it's because of machines. They're dehumanising us. But John Buchan blames the war. He says we've lost our balance."

The detective remarked idly, "I'm surprised John Buchan gets read in your Russian Tearooms."

"Every argument needs opposition, sir. A lot has been said about those tearooms, sir, but I heard an awful lot of sense in there. And they say that we should read the likes of Mr Buchan so that we can understand the folly of it. It all gets explained, you see."

The detective kept quiet. He wasn't comfortable in conversation with left thinking policemen.

"Have you read his Island of Sheep, sir? It's got the best motor chase in any book in our local Boots."

The police car stopped outside a city centre pub and Turncott, in a brown suit with matching brogues and trilby, collected his case from the boot before walking in for a pint.

Willis provoked a brief commotion by turning in the road. He was heading directly out of the city. He knew better than to expect a warm welcome in any local police station so, promising himself an afternoon tea on the Hog's Back, he headed out of the city without a stop. His business here was done.

Chief Inspector Turncott stood at the bar with his suitcase at his feet and downed two mild and bitters without a word. He liked the smell of workmen's tobacco. It had a rawness that you couldn't get from refined cigarettes and its good, grey colour seemed as natural as wood smoke. He pretended to be absorbed by a hand painted frieze of a fleet review. The line of ships stretched from one end of the bar to the other. A man in a cloth cap thought about talking to him but Turncott wasn't a man you could easily engage in chatter. He liked to listen. A group of Navy reservists were discussing the call up and, round the corner, a woman in a paisley patterned headscarf was making excuses for expectant fathers who went off the rails. Apparently, young Fairclough from Adelaide Street had done just that, but his woman couldn't think bad of him. "Nor should she," insisted the man in the cloth cap.

Turncott smiled when he heard some gossip about the city's policemen. 'Sergeant' Gutterman could be found, most nights, locked in the Red Cow after hours.

The woman called across from the bar. "They're getting fatty. Have you seen that?"

"Aye, and balder too!"

"Most of them are!" the woman cried. "Most of them are."

"It'll get worse as the young'uns join up for the fighting. We'll be left with crocks for rossers who should be on the second-hand market, by rights."

"They'll be no fighting," said a voice from the back. "No war at all. Mark the words of an old soldier. Never again, our subalterns were saying all the time. We'd be cradling a Tommy with his foot blown off and the subbies would promise 'never again, never again'. And now, you see, those subalterns are generals, so they'll be no war. They'll stop it."

"And what if war's the right thing?" queried the woman.

But Turncott heard no mention of the Wycherley Murder. He stood, smoking a Weights at the bar until the men started to talk about football faggies. Then he slipped away, quietly but not unnoticed. They judged him, 'From London. And Government, no doubt. He weren't selling. You can tell a man who's done no selling.'

He left the road of busy shops behind him, passed under the bridge of the Town Railway Station and walked through the terraces where well-to-do people had lived fifty years before. Now, the homes had been converted into offices for solicitors, architects and grand-sounding doctors. A locomotive rattled overhead, disgorging smoke and fumes like bad indigestion – and Turncott understood why the posh people had found better places to live. When he saw a grey-haired policeman standing at a crossroads, the detective steadied his pace. But the copper was too clever; he sensed that the man in brown clothes was a superior officer so he smartened up, saluted a nanny with a perambulator, and slow marched round a corner.

Turncott carried his suitcase along a side street of one-mechanic garages, outfitters who displayed cheap and shoddy clothes on the pavement, and grocer shops with muddy potatoes. He found the front door of Number 83 between a barber and a wicker shop. Brooms and baskets and chairs with raffia seats hung from an awning.

"She'll not be in," warned a youngster on a scooter.

He placed the suitcase at his feet, stood on the step and knocked loudly.

"I can hear you!"

But no-one came to the door.

He knocked again.

"I said I can hear. You'll have police round, banging like that." A face appeared at the parlour curtains. She was tucking the last fingers of hair into the bun.

At last, Miss Ditchen came to the door. "You've come about the murder."

"No, I've come about the room."

"But the murder's why you're here."

"Can I come in, Rosie?"

"Buttermilk's sent you. 'Go down and get a room with Rosie,' he'll have said. 'Get her to tell you all about it.' Well, you tell Buttermilk Dolby that this Rosie Ditchen doesn't work for him anymore. You tell him, he stops bothering her or this Rosie will tell everything she knows."

"Rosie, there's nothing to worry about. Please, let me indoors."

Miss Ditchen lived in a terrace house of small rooms with heavy curtains and brown furniture. She kept the place warm – she was careful to leave the kitchen door open if the oven was on, and she kept fires in the sitting-room and, after five, in her bedroom. Again, she left the door open so that the fire would warm the landing. She told her visitor to leave his suitcase at the foot of the stairs and, having hung his hat and coat in a cupboard, placed him in an armchair at the hearth while she busied herself in the kitchen.

"Goodness me, Rosie," he called. "Have you been baking cakes?"

"Because of that Elsie."

"The one they call Big Elsie?"

"Never mind about her," Rosie grumbled. And they didn't speak again until she wheeled a tea trolley into the parlour.

"She's told everyone that I'll never be able to turn out a bun as tastily as she does and even if I did, who would I share it with? She's always saying that, that I'm lonely and sad and got no-one. Well, I'll tell you, I may not have a fishie sea captain and a fresh faced policeman in my house or a husband who's gone off to Lord knows where, but I do know some good people and I did learn to cook, once. Maybe not when I was at school with Elsie and Annie and the others. But later, when I worked in a school kitchen."

"Yes," said Turncott as he arranged a cake and a little fork on his pretty plate. "You were a school maid, weren't you?"

"Before I realised that it was a mistake to leave hereabouts. Then I came back."

"Tell me, what did Mr Wycherley say to you before he died?"

"What's that got to do with my cakes?"

"It's why I'm here, Rosie. You said as much. He gave you some papers, didn't he?"

"No. He had some papers with him." She took a sip of tea, swallowed it and checked that the corners of her lips were clean. "But I don't know where they are now."

"Oh no, Rosie. You didn't lose them. No-one believes that. You're too good at your job to do that."

"It's not my job," she insisted. "I told you, I don't work for Buttermilk anymore."

Turncott allowed that. "So, what did Mr Wycherley say about the papers?"

"Only that I was to study them carefully. But I didn't. They were gone as soon as he was killed. The killer took them, I should think."

"Oh, yes. I think so too. But you know what was in them?"

"Of course, I do. Everyone does."

"He'd found a weakness in the city's air defence, hadn't he?" Turncott smiled. "He used to walk along the cliffs and draw things so that he could work it all out. And, that night, he brought the answers to the pub and told you to look after them."

"But I didn't. You can tell Mr Buttermilk that I lost them."

"But you didn't lose them," Turncott argued forcibly. "You've got them still and when you're sure it's the right thing to do, you'll give them to me."

"No. I've not got them."

"Who was there, Rosie? Who was there to murder Mr Wycherley and steal the secret papers?"

"Mrs Ritchers and me downstairs and Soapy Berkeley in the meeting room, up top."

"And no-one else?"

"Shaking Jacobs was supposed to be there but now he says he wasn't."

"And silly Annie?"

"You leave Annie out of this," Rosie snapped. "She's a good girl. She's poor. She lives in a charity cottage and her husband's no good to her anymore."

She saw that Turncott wanted to laugh.

"Does that make her good, Rosie? Because she's poor?"

"Well, you leave her alone."

"Why?"

Because poor Annie can't tell fibs, but Rosie wasn't going to say that. She recalled how children had called Annie 'the canary' at school because she was always telling tales to the teachers. 'No-one sings like our Annie Canary,' they chanted. Rosie looked at Turncott and said, "You're a horrid man."

"Do you remember anything else?"

"His footsteps on the stairs. It was like he was a condemned man walking to his death."

"You didn't think that at the time."

"No, but it made me think of a church bell going bong-bong in the desert. I thought, 'It tolls for a lost soul.' I did think that, really. I remembered another bell. God, thinking of it still sends me cold. When I was a young woman working in that boarding school." She kept her eyes down as she spoke. "I was just a kitchen maid, as you said, and I used to sleep in. Whenever a boy was due to be beaten, after bedtime, the school bell used to toll in a tower. It was that same horrible ragged rhythm. Like the church bell in a desert. And when the ringing stopped, we all knew that the beating had begun. Horrible, it was. Listening to that bell. Marching to death, just as Wycherley was doing on the Palfreyman's stairs. It's a signal that something wicked is going to happen, something that mankind hasn't learned to get the better of. That's how things are now, you know. We're all marching to another war and we mustn't allow it. Otherwise, it will get the better of us. I don't mean Germany. I mean the war. The war would overcome us all. That's why we must have peace. Peace at any price."

Turncott laid his hands open on his knees, ready for her to take if she wanted. "I know Rosie, and each of us must do what we can to stop it. But, sometimes, we can't listen to the people who are trying to drive us, can we? Sometimes, we have to do what is right."

She lifted her head. "You're not working for Buttermilk, are you? He didn't send you here at all."

"Now, don't you worry about that. You know, I don't want you to give me the papers just now. It's better that you think about it and give them to me when you're sure it's the right thing to do."

But Miss Rosemary Ditchen was clever. This man had been sent to trick her but Rosie would turn the tables. Oh my word, she would. That evening – when he was out on the streets and she was making up his bed in the second guest room – she pictured herself, making sure of each step. "Coming here," she muttered as she turned back the sheets. "Coming here and thinking he can make a fool of me. Well, Rosie'll teach him a lesson. Oh yes, I'll teach him one of Rosie's best lessons." She tilted the shade on the table lamp. She nudged the dressing table mirror. "I'll tempt him," she said. Yes, that's what she would do. Tempt him and get him so confused that he wouldn't know whose side he was on.

SIX

A Night Patrol

On a damp Tuesday evening in October – not twenty-four hours after the murder of Hubert Wycherley and the night before the second body in the case – a patrol of eight officers marched from their grey stone police station and faced a cold drizzle. PCs Smith and Benson were at the front. Tiny Talbot and I made a little and large pair in the second row. Then came two officers from another division, while Sergeant Martindale kept pace with Lancaster and Stride at the back. The sergeant had already reminded us of the crimes and nuisances on our beats. "The detective at Central is interested in any vehicles leaving the freight yard after two o'clock," he had told me. "Note down the details of any you see. And don't forget the noises behind Mrs Oakley's place. She's old but that doesn't mean she's daft." In the muster room, he had read out a list of unoccupied properties and detailed PC Talbot to check the boxes at the traffic lights at one o'clock. "Or thereabouts, Tiny. Good man." Then he had called the parade to attention and required us to 'present our appointments' before he marched us out.

We had not reached the first street corner when a weedy chap in a cloth cap celebrated our approach by whistling the Laurel and Hardy theme. "Deal with him," barked the sergeant. Lancaster and Stride broke away from the patrol, took an arm each and carried the little fellow into the station.[5] "Eyes front, Mr Machray. There's nothing worse than a constable treading in dog muck." At Kirten Street, the

---

5 In 1944, I met Willy Stainer in a Cambridgeshire pub. He told me that he spent a couple of hours in a police cell that night. He knew better than to complain. Any protest would have prompted a charge of drunk and disorderly.

third row peeled off to the right. Once free of the patrol, their pace slackened and, when they separated at the end of the road, they slowed to a dawdle. "You're next Mr Machray," he warned. We all knew that he had assigned me to Goodladies Road so that I couldn't snoop around Cathedral Close or risk tea and muffins in Elsie's kitchen. "Your points are ten-past at the blue box and twenty-to at the kiosk on Cardrew Street. Don't mix them up. Half hour refs at one o'clock – find your own 'stop'; I don't want to see you back in the station until morning. Off you go, lad."

When, three weeks before, Sergeant Martindale had shown me Goodladies Road for the first time, he pointed out the traders and their premises and our best ways of keeping an eye on them. "Climb the wrought iron staircase outside Stott's bakery and you can observe Goodladies Junction and as far west as the railway lines. And Mitre Passage is across the road; stand in the crook of its dog leg and you'll hear everything that goes on in the builder's yard. No-one can tell you're there, so it's a beauty." Then he told me about Mr Haraldson, the watchmaker. "Round here, they call him Swiss Made. His light is on well into the night. He works late, you see, so check on him. Make sure he's all right. Always look out for the lonely men who work too hard; they're easy pickings for the scoundrels. Keep in step, lad. Do try. Ma Shipley in her cafe, she knows most of what's happening. Take your refs there and she'll see you right. And keep an eye on young Davy Tupner; he sells dirty drawings for his dad and no-one's too happy about him." I asked where I could find him. "In the old Methodist porch or the wood shelters beneath Warne's warehouse. Come on, I'll show you. Hey, slow down, lad. A good policeman never gets wet and he never runs. He proceeds, and proceeding doesn't include running. Do try and keep in step, though."

The sergeant had given me good advice, but I knew that I wouldn't get to grips with the place until I had walked Goodladies Road on my own. Pavements at the bottom end – where buses turn and cinema queues spill onto the road – were crowded with people in hats and coats; the second house was about to open and three late buses had pulled in at the same time.

Everyone looked drab in greys and browns. It seemed that all the collars were up and all the hats turned down so that it was difficult to distinguish the faces. There was a little banter – 'Hey, behave yourself, Tom Cartwright, or the nice policeman will run you in!' – but no-one paid much attention to me. In fact, most people seemed to be staring down at the pavements; even those walking across the road from the buses didn't look properly where they were going. Then, as I watched from a shop porch, a woman emerged from the tide of people. Other folk slowed down, allowing a path for her. Women looked, even more than the men, and envied her cool, unhurried progress. She moved with an easy rhythm – as if she were stepping to music in her head. She wasn't fancily dressed; she wore a twin set, a thin jumper and cardigan beneath a well worn two piece suit. None of it looked new. She had left her coat open, which might have been to show off so the girls might have called her tarty. But I didn't see that. I thought she was 'expert'. (That was a word from the latest radio serial.) She had dressed for pennies but the lets and tucks in her clothes made the most of her every movement. Or perhaps she made the outfit work in a special way. She swayed, just a little. She tossed her head, just a hint of it, so that it all had the touch of a Latin dance, but she did everything without a noise.

"Irish Dowell," a voice croaked behind me. "Prime stuff. Unsalted, unsmoked, just very slightly cooked by one or two."

I said without thinking, "Her mother isn't Irish at all."

"Neither's she."

I looked over my shoulder. Soapy Berkeley, a dirty weasel of a character, was fidgeting in his pockets. "It's going to rain," he said. "It's going to rain hard. What'd you give to look up her dresses?"

"Don't be filthy."

"Go on, though. What'd you give?"

He was short, with an old suit slipping off his spindly frame, a coarse complexion and pits on the backs of his hands. He didn't work; his dress, his shuffle and slouch, his sloppy speech and the emptiness in his eyes bore the stain of unemployment. But I couldn't feel sorry for him.

"Where'd you get to on the night Wycherley died?" I asked.

"You want me to tell you here? In a shop door with loads of folk passing by? And it's going to rain, anyway."

I took him to a cafe at the traffic lights. The weather had broken before we got in and the floor got muddier with every new customer. Soon, the rain was so hard that the cafe windows misted and we couldn't properly see the motorcars at the crossroads.

"Go on," Berkeley said, stirring his tea continuously. "I'll tell you where I was but you've got to tell me first."

"Me? I was at Elsie's."

"Not that," he persisted, now paddling the spoon as if he were folding butter into a tasty dish. "You've got to tell me what you'd give to look up Irish Dowell's dress."

"Don't be stupid."

"Then I won't tell you where I was."

I wasn't comfortable. I shifted on my chair and tried to stretch the seat of my trousers. "Look, I'm a policeman."

He corrected me. "No, no. You're a policeman who doesn't know where I was when Bert Wycherley died. That means you want me to talk. So that's what you are – a policeman who needs to do business with Soapy Berkeley." He looked at the way I was sitting. "Most people can't keep still when they meet me. They worry that I'll give them fleas. But you're different. There's something wrong with you, isn't there?" He leaned forward, waited for the words to come to the very front of his mouth, then he asked, "You got spots?"

"I'm just a little sore," I admitted. "Too much cycling in one day. I'm not used to it."

His weasel face perked up. "What'd you find out?"

"Nothing," I said. "I mean, I wasn't looking for anything. Look, I'm not sure I should be sitting in here when I'm on duty."

"Of course you should," he drawled. "The owner likes it. A copper in the place keeps everyone in order."

I checked my watch.

"Don't worry about your point. Look, no copper could walk up Goodladies Road without getting a job. You're on an 'enquiry'; it's as simple as that. Tell them Soapy Berkeley had something important to tell you. Now, where were we? Oh, yes, we were inside 'Eyrie' Dowell's dress."

"No, you're going to tell me where you were when Bert Wycherley died."

"Lord, I was in the room. You know that. And Mr Gutterman's

had me in for questioning and he's very happy with what I told him. Very happy, he said. Look, I was standing at the window, calling down to coalman Sid as it happened, as poor Bertie fell into the room. He must have been walloped by someone who was following him, or someone waiting for him on the landing. I didn't see, because I was looking out of the window. Anyway, I turned around and, aghast that he was dead, I was aghast, I jumped down to Sid's cart."

"Where did you go?"

"You got a lot of questions, Mr Machray, for a copper who's doing no more than walking up and down Goodladies Road. I hid round the back of the Hoboken, matter of fact. I was in the kitchen until gone one o'clock, then they threw me out. Threatened to turn me in, they did."

"Why wasn't Shaking Jacobs with you when Wycherley arrived?"

"I said to Mr Gutterman, 'that's a very good question'. I'd spend a lot of time on that question, if I was you. Either one of you, I would."

With that, Berkeley walked out on me and the cafe owner, with tea cloths over his shoulder, round his neck and tucked in his waist, came to clear our table. "The pretty young lady they call Irish. Let me explain. Her name is Iris but she is drunk so much of the time that they make fun of her and call her Irish. Because that's how she says her name when she is tipsy. 'Irisshh.' Are you our new policeman?" he asked. "Then you sit here for as long as you like. I tell all my customers that the policemen are very welcome in here. If you don't want to sit with a policeman, don't come. Are you worried about the time? Please, your sergeant knows where you are, don't worry about him. If you must call him, please use my telephone behind the counter."

I left my helmet on the table and, all through the phone call, I was anxious about it. A copper's first rule was to look after his hat. 'Mark my words, lad. Scallywags will want to pinch it and, if you let them, they'll poke fun at you for years.' I stood behind the counter and didn't take my eyes of it. On this occasion no-one tried to humiliate me but I was beginning to doubt that I'd ever make a good policeman. I couldn't get even the simple things right.

The desk officer knew where I was calling from. He also knew that 'Soapy' Berkeley had taken me there. He made a joke of it – it was the sort of trap that every newcomer walks into – and he promised to cover for me. "I've a job for you, Eddie. Young David Tupner is selling his father's postcards at the dead end of Rossington Street. Ask to see his pedlar's certificate. He'll promise to go home for it but we'll see no more of him this evening. That'll do. Don't make more of it. Young David means no harm."

Most of the addresses on 'the road' were business premises. Shadowy carriage agents. Grubby offices of those firms that buy and sell things abroad (though they couldn't have been doing much trade in those years before the war). And useful small shops with their wares on the pavements. But I was surprised by the number of families who made their homes in these houses. At first I thought that it must have been a noisy life, but the more I watched, the more I realised that the sounds of the traffic, the shouting and crashing about weren't a nuisance to people who lived here. They loved the busyness. A troublesome horse, an awkward load that needed twelve passers-by to successfully reverse it into a yard, the hammering that no-one could source but everyone put up with – these little episodes of chaos were the stuff of daily life and contentment to folk in this neighbourhood. No-one seemed to sleep, unless it was in grandma's chair in a front doorway. And even when the thoroughfare quietened down, usually between midnight and one, there were sufficient eyes at the corners of windows or in the shadows of the jitties to let a man know that he might go about his business without tales being told but he would never go unnoticed.

As I started to proceed towards Rossington Street, a figure emerged from the shadows. "How did you get on with the Dep's wife?" he said as he fell in with my step.

"I didn't get a cup of tea out of her,"

"No, no," he laughed. "No, I shouldn't have thought so. Sal Devonshire's got no time for young PCs. Perhaps you fared better at the Chief Constable's place?"

I knew I was talking to the Scotland Yarder. "Not much. I dug up the wrong flower bed and she caught me pinching a nutty biscuit." I looked sideways at him. "I'm not sure she mentioned the biscuit."

"You have an able Chief Constable, young man. He is at the end of his career and, granted, he's not as sharp as he was. But you need to remember what he's been through. He rode on horseback into the battles of the South African War and even had his favourite mount shot from under him. In his day, you would have met few braver men and he was a true patriot, not like the fair-weather merchants we've got now."

"And he's got a pretty wife."

"Yes," he said and paused to eye me suspiciously. "Yes, he's been well catered for. Come on, we'll take a walk through alleyways."

When we were out of sight, he stopped in the shadow where two back fences met. He rolled two cigarettes. He passed one to me and offered a light.

"Mr Machray, I'm a professional policeman. People say that I'm staid and old fashioned; I don't think so. I like to be adventurous, mischievous even, in the way I do the job and I don't expect detectives to comply with the rules. Why should officers be congratulated for doing what others tell them? But I've no time for policemen who don't do their job. And that means two things – staying close to the people and not turning away from things that are wrong."

As he spoke, we listened to a family argument that spilled from a back door.

"I've little patience with these new bobbies in motors," he continued, "or on horses or at the top end of dog lead. More than once I've shouted at them in the street, 'Get out of your car' – or down from your horse or away from that lead- 'and come down to people's level.' And I've been told off for making a scene. Now you, you're lazy and ham-fisted and we'll fall out about that. But I'll give you a chance because you allow time for the ordinary chap on your beat. That's what you were doing last night when the Chief couldn't find you. God in heaven!" He laughed. "They'd had one murder and then they couldn't find their beat bobby for four hours!" (I saw that Turncott had a familiar Met attitude to provincial detectives.)

"But they'd written it in the book," I pleaded. "'Written off to detectives, the man on the desk said."

He jerked his finger to the noise over the fence. "Who's winning the argument?"

"They keep mentioning Soapy Berkeley," I said.

"And David Tupner, the lad you were supposed to chase from Rossington Street."

"The husband will have to give in," I said. "Mother's in charge of children."

"She thinks he's popped it, that's the trouble. She thinks he's popped his lad's new jacket."

"I'll walk past in an hour or so," I said.

"Who's out there!" shouted the mother. "Maurice, there's someone on the other side of our fence!"

Then Turncott spoke about my uncle and I made it clear that I had very little to do with the man. Yes, he'd suggested the police as a promising profession, but I expected no special consideration because of a family connection. When Turncott seemed pleased with that reaction, I went further. "I don't want anybody to expect me to be as outstanding a policeman as my uncle was. Firstly, I'll be no good at this lark, I know that now, and I can't see me standing it for more than a year. There's going to be a war and I want to be part of it. I don't want to be pounding pavements when my country needs defending."

"What's wrong?" he said seriously. "What's so very wrong," and he looked me in the eyes, "with pounding a pavement?"

I thought it was an absurd question and chose not to answer it properly. "I've been a policeman for six months," I said. "And I don't know what I'm doing here. I'm not suited to a job that treats me like a soldier."

"You'll get suited soon enough, if there's a war," he argued reasonably.

"And the shift work; it makes me eat when I'm not hungry and makes me work when I want to eat. My stomach doesn't know what time of day it is."

"You'll get used to that."

"And working at weekends means there are less weeks in a year."

"So Christmas comes round quicker."

"Yes. Yes, I suppose so. But what's this nonsense about turning up for work fifteen minutes before your wages started."

"Many jobs do. We're not so peculiar in that, are we?"

"Well, it's another gripe."

He said, "But, of course, when you are out of the station and you're off the leash, it's not work, is it?" Then he cleverly got to the nub of my discontent. "Where are you living?"

"I'm with Big Elsie and I'm, sort of, uneasy about that. She mothers me and that's fine. I mean, I need that, don't I? It means my clothes are always done and there's good food on my plate. But she, kind of, shows off."

"Shows off?"

"Let's me see bits of her and pretends it's an accident."

I knew it was a funny story but Turncott kept his amusement to himself. He offered no advice, so I said, "I've asked Sergeant Somers if I can stay in the Palfreyman or the Hoboken but he says the Chief Constable might not approve of a constable with digs in a pub. So, with the section house closed and no other private lodgings on the books, I'm stuck. I think Mr Somers suggested that Sergeant Martindale should give me a beat away from Elsie's place."

He drew breath. "You're right. When war comes, there'll have other jobs for you but, until then, give this job a couple of years before you throw your hand in."

Then the back gate opened and a man with no jacket, open boots and trousers loose at the waist appeared before us. "You heard all that, I suppose," he said. "She says I've got to get our Mark's best coat back. So what are you going to do about it?"

He told us that Davy Tupner had been 'selling Bible words' to their middle son.

"I can't stop people preaching," I said.

"But he told the kid to give things to the poor. So he did, he gave Tupner his best coat for Soapy Berkeley."

"Surely not? It wouldn't fit."

"But Tupner tells the lad it'll do fine. Soapy can sell it."

Turncott, a smile on his face, was waiting for my reaction. It was like another test to see if I was a good policeman.

"I'll get the coat back for you, sir," I said and the man went back to his scullery, calling, "Did you hear that, Martha. The new bobby says he'll have it all sorted before morning."

"Well, he just better!" the wife yelled from the sink.

Neighbours shouted from their bedrooms and back door steps. "You tell him, Martha." "Yes, tell him 'or what'. What'll you do, Martha?"

Turncott waited for the laughter and calling out to settle, then he asked, "Why did you search Wycherley's rooms?" When I hesitated, he added quietly, "Rosie Ditchen saw you. About twenty past eleven, she says."

"That would be right. I wanted to find out why he had gone to the Palfreyman. He'd taken a sheath of papers with him but they were missing. I thought I might get a clue from the papers he'd left at home. I'm sorry that Miss Ditchen saw me. I thought I was more careful than that."

"What did you find?"

"His sketchbook. Wycherley had spent hours at a secluded part of the coast. I thought I recognised the scene so I cycled over there today."

"And you found?" he repeated.

"A pit. Or something like a pit, concealed from the beach but not too far from it. I wondered if it was something to do with smuggling or illegal gambling. Bare knuckle fighting, do you think?"

"Or a witch's coven?"

"I looked for any signs of a bonfire or ritual goings-on but –" I shook my head. "I'm only guessing."

"But you believe this cauldron had something to do with Wycherley's death."

"I'm sure the place occupied his last days. It could be dog fighting."

That interested him. "What makes you say that?"

"It was the same shape as other pits I've seen." Nonsense, but I wasn't going to mention that a child had put the idea in my head.

"And today's jaunt was just an off duty cycle ride?"

I said, "I knew you'd be watching me." But I hadn't thought that Miss Ditchen was the Chief Inspector's spy. "Sir, I think we need to turn the evidence on its head."

"PC Machray," he said.

"Yes sir."

"You talk nonsense."

"Yes sir."

"Do you think that the Commissioner would send me down here settle a feud between dog fighters? Hubert Wycherley had uncovered mistakes in our national security."

We didn't speak for ten minutes. I went with him to the end of the alley, where he found an open shed at the back of one of the houses. It had no tools in it; it looked like a wooden shelter for someone who wanted to keep out of the way. We smoked more cigarettes and listened to the noises of a neighbourhood closing down for the night. Cats and rubbish being put out into yards. Doors being locked. Sinks emptied. Tired people climbing the stairs.

"It's not chance that I'm lodging with Miss Ditchen," he said. "Your uncle used to work for a man called Dolby. 'Buttermilk' Dolby. He heads one of the departments that look after security on the home front."

"The spycatchers!" I said like they do in the pictures.

He sighed. "Unfortunately, there are so many different spy-catching services that we fall over one another."

"I don't have much to do with my uncle," I said.

"Rosie Ditchen was another of Buttermilk's agents; she stopped working with him twelve months ago. She said it was too risky. She was scared of it all. Yesterday, we told her that I'd take a room in her house because it was safe and she was trustworthy. But Buttermilk's unsure of her, that's the truth, and he's right to be suspicious. PC Machray, I want you to uncover evidence to prove that Rosie Ditchen killed Hubert Wycherley."

"We don't know that she did," I protested. "When Wycherley was murdered in the Palfreyman, Rosie Ditchen was downstairs in the saloon bar. She'd been there for an hour and she even refused to leave when the Mrs Ritchers asked her to call for me."

"Yes, it's a good alibi. I want you to break it. Constable, I know a killer when I see one. Crike man, I'm living with this woman, aren't I? And that's why I have to rely on you to convict her. I'm too close; we can't let her see what I'm up to." But he saw that I was reluctant. "Look, she tells lies. She says that she hasn't got Wycherley's plans but I know she has." He took my arm. "Machray, it may be that I'll need you to do a job without it going in your pocket book."

"I'll not perjure myself," I said.

"No. But I may need you to recover the documents in secret."

"Steal them?"

"I said recover them, Mr Machray. But tell no-one about it."

I hesitated. "Perhaps I'm not experienced enough," I said.

He watched me closely. "No. Perhaps not. Perhaps it's wise to keep you out of this."

He stepped away, but turned back to say, "I'm not being unfair in this. Look, I shouldn't tell you. There is a story that Rosie Ditchen has killed before. It's always denied. These things are and quite rightly so, I say. Before I came down here, I went to my Commissioner and demanded to know the truth. He told me there was absolutely no truth in the rumour. None at all. But the story is there. People do say it."

He walked on, leaving me in the wooden shelter. I pictured the saloon bar on the night of the murder. I pictured the car mechanic rushing in and telling how Soapy Berkeley had jumped from the window. I imagined someone running down the stairs to shout 'Murder!' And then, they all went to see the body. Leaving Rosie Ditchen alone in the bar. Yes, Hubert Wycherley was already dead but, for several minutes close to the murder, Rosie Ditchen was alone in the Palfreyman, without a witness.

I remembered Annie's advice in the middle of that first night. 'If Rosie's made a mistake, let her make up for it.' So, what had Rosie Ditchen done that could only be put right by Hubert Wycherley's death? It had something to do with the house on the cliff. And it was something that Turncott wanted to clear up quickly.

I was a long way from making any sense of it.

It had past eleven when Turncott and I parted. I walked back to the main road and started the patrol that would occupy me for the rest of the night. The Hoboken Arms had emptied. Lovers were spooning in back porches or beneath the streetlights in the side roads. A widower and his dog were on a ten-minute walk before settling down. Recently, the BBC had started to broadcast from the Savoy again and the 'slippers and armchair music' of Geraldo's orchestra drifted from behind every fourth or fifth set of curtains. At the corner of Goodladies and Cardrew Street, two children peeped from an upstairs window. I smiled as I remembered how Elsie had once described the families on Goodladies Road. There are only two types, she insisted. Those who have too many children and let them take over main bedroom at the front, and those who make them squeeze more tightly into the back room. She made no allowance for those who had put-me-ups in the parlour. And I knew one family where sleeping at the top of the staircase was a treat allowed to the best behaved children of seven.[6]

As I turned into Rossington Street, I caught the vibrant sound of a ukulele. The youth called Davy Tupner had his ankles crossed as he leant against a lamp-post at the dead end. His spiv's hat was cocked to one side and an inane smile clung to his face like plasticine. He didn't move on but watched me walk along the hundred yards of pavement.

"What are you doing?" I asked.

"Do you want me to sing it?"

"No, I don't."

His fingers went on rattling over the strings producing music that, frankly, was better than his foolish face deserved. "I could show you my new flicker, if you want." He was wearing a dog tooth jacket and trousers that had been sewn at home on a wobbly machine. The sleeves and legs turned up two inches before they needed to.

"Stop playing!"

He slowed down and went more quietly and, when he judged that my patience was at an end, he tucked the ukulele under his arm and produced a pocket book from the back of his trousers. "Look, you flick through the pages and the pictures move."

"Where's Mark's best jacket?" I asked.

"Look," he leaned forward and worked the novelty again. "See, Malcolm Campbell's Bluebird speeding at more than four hundred miles an hour."

"The jacket?"

"I've got it," he said and kicked a cloth bag at his feet.

6 Years later, Timberdick insisted that Mums and Dads moved to the back room so that people on the street wouldn't hear them making love. I doubt that. The houses were so small, with only two rooms upstairs, that well mannered people got used to doing things quietly.

"You sold it to Soapy Berkeley."

"No, I didn't. I kept it for myself because it's got a secret pocket sewn into the lining. For keeping a knife in. So I kept it."

"I want you to give it back," I said.

"Don't you want to see my pedlar's chit?"

"No, I don't. Give it to me and I'll do it."

He put the pocket book away and sulked as he handed over the cloth bag. "It's not even his best jacket. It's second-hand. It smells of fish so he probably got it off the boats. And his name's not Louis Bloire so it can't have been properly his."

"Louis Bloire? Why are you telling me this?"

"The name's in the collar. That's all I'm saying."

When I got back to the alley, the house was locked up and the lights were off, so I tied a police luggage label to the handle of the bag and left it on the doorstep.

* * *

Unspoilt mist came in from the sea and, through gaps in the streets, crept between houses and shops. It was twenty past six, I was off duty and walking slowly towards my digs. I had put a gabardine over my uniform shirt and within ten minutes it was damp and my face tingled with icy moisture. The tobacconist had been pressing me to call in for a mug of tea so, seeing that the downstairs light was on, I rattled the back door.

"Hey! People here are good," he cheered. "They like their good tobacco and they don't care where the shopkeeper was born."

I guessed it hadn't always been that way. "The kid's don't get any trouble?" I asked.

"Now, it's always the kiddies. People say bad things about my girls but they say it behind our backs. But always, for the kids, yeah, it's close up to the face. Hey, who can change kids?"

I said, maybe, it had something to do with a seaport. People were used to comings and goings. But we both recognised that I had introduced another question and we laid it aside.

I was sitting in the cubby hole between the Teggs' kitchen and their coal shed. Rennie Teggs – scrubbed up, brushed and rosy clean

– was standing on the step but kept going back to the kitchen to do things or answer his wife or hurry his daughter. "She has to be at work – fifteen minutes to eight, but she dresses so carefully as if she parades before the boys. Ned, I give up."

He disappeared. I heard his wife shouting for the young ones to keep out of Mariella's way.

Then Rennie came back with half a slice of bread, dipped it egg and fried. (It was cooked like this so that one egg could treat three people.) "I have been reading the editor of one of your monthlies. He's very good." He sat on the stone step and dropped the magazine in my lap. Teggs had learned English ten years ago by reading magazines and he believed that an hour each week with his head bent over newsprint would keep him up to scratch. "He says he's sick. Sick of hearing about the Prince and Mrs Simpson, sick of seeing Tommy Farr's photograph – he makes a joke 'the posters are sometimes near, but they are always Farr' – and he's sick of seeing Robert Taylor's hairy chest. Good, don't you think?"

"You've cut a page out," I said.

"Yes, it's on the shop wall. An advertisement for De Rezke Minors. A tin of thirty cigarettes for only a bob. The company's representative will like to see it on our wall. He'll say, 'Aha! Mr Teggs is on the ball again!' There's another in there you'll like."

At first I wasn't sure what he meant, but when I turned the pages I found a sketch promoting Greys fags. "Good grief!" I shrieked.

"No, no. Please, the family mustn't see it."

A woman was drawn in her bath, holding one shapely leg and two arms high in the air. She had found the cigarettes and matches that she had lost in the water. But the cigarettes had been kept dry by a 'patent hermetically sealed carton'. The joke hadn't surprised me, but I couldn't believe the extent of the bosom that was on show. "Grief, Teggs, look! It's all there!" And, like two schoolboys in a corner of the playground, we giggled over the saucy caricature.

"What is all this?" his wife asked as she walked into the kitchen.

"No. Nothing." I closed the magazine.

"Really? What are you looking at out there? Let me see."

"The advertisements for the RAF," fibbed Teggs. By now, his wife was at his shoulder and Teggs knew that he had to keep talking.

"Our Ned is sad because he's a year too old to be an unskilled recruit. And I was saying, 'Ned, you must be a policeman like your uncle.' He has a famous uncle, don't you know." He emphasised, "A top-notch policeman. 'A Top Notch,' is that it?" He laughed, "Perhaps, he is a spy."

I said I had very little to do with my uncle.

"Ned, people round here, they like you." He took the magazine and sat on it. "They say, 'Ned's our copper.' So I'm telling you this. Perhaps one day I'll need a copper and you'll remember. So I'm telling you what I've heard. Your boss, the detective from Scotland Yard, he's not playing straight with you."

His wife walked away. "Maybe I should read this Popular Flying before I go to sleep tonight," she said. "You'll leave it on my pillow, my dear heart."

"What have you heard about Mr Turncott?" I asked.

"Sometimes, I think it's best to keep up to date with what men are reading in this house," the woman teased from the kitchen.

Teggs said loudly, "My friend and I are talking seriously." Then he leaned towards me. "Yesterday, he went to the dockyard and he was asking many questions. What has all this business to do with the Air Raid Precautions? But you want to know about dog fighting? What man who can tell you about this? I can tell you, Ned, you are looking for the right man and he is hiding in the filthy alley behind the waterfront. The house has no number but a square in a diamond is painted on the back wall."

"Who am I looking for, Mr Teggs?"

"I don't know," he replied with a theatrical shrug. "I don't even know if it's true. I am telling you only what I've overheard. Some people, they think my English is only so-so and this makes them talk more freely."

Then a rumble came over the houses of Goodladies Road, making roof tiles shake and locks shudder. With me, Teggs craned his neck as a huge aeroplane flew low and slowly over the cathedral. So majestic, so profound that the crows didn't scatter from the cathedral tower; I think that they were so thunderstruck that they watched, like us. We saw it lift and bank perilously as the pilot turned towards the sea. "I've never seen such an aeroplane," I said, unable to disguise my patriotism. Its low height had emphasised the blatant, vulgar size of the thing.

"It's the new bomber," said Teggs. (He emphasised the second 'b' – 'bom-ber') "The Armstrong Whitely. It must be one of the very first; even now, your RAF does not want to talk very much about it. Seventy feet long."

In too few years we would become accustomed to seeing glass turrets on top, beneath and at each end of our bombers, but my first sight of this great ship of the sky – a truly flying fortress – with its 'greenhouses' at the front and the tail, was awesome. The muddy green and brown colours made it so different from the silver aircraft that I was used to seeing. This one wasn't meant to shine or remind people of the stars in heaven. It wasn't meant to impress us by winning races or showing off at air pageants. The camouflage, more than anything, said that this great bulwark had been built to do work. She was sleek, thunderous and ready for war. "England will be well defended," I said. "With chariots like that, no-one will dare touch us."

"Ah, no, my friend. The bomber defends no-one. She is for wiping out the enemy. We have seen what bombers do to cities in Spain."

I didn't reply for a few moments. I knew that the newsreels still spoke of the hell brought to Guernica just a few months before; it was a terrible premonition of things to come. Quietly, I turned to face him and said, "It's your RAF too, you know. Not just 'my' RAF. England welcomes everyone who comes to her shores."

SEVEN

My Affair with the Girl in the Loft

A hard working harbour struggled beneath a damp and dirty sky. Everything had a gunmetal look, something to do with reflections of clouds in mud coloured water and belches of grey smoke from the chimneys. Like tarnished pewter. Working men struggled on. Laden women with aching backs and swollen feet didn't complain; they kept their troubles to themselves.

The masters were moving steamers about the harbour – paddle steamers, tugs, the busy little harbour ferries and sooted freighters bound for the Empire. I got the taste from the smoke-stacks as I cycled over the level crossing of the Admiralty railway. Wary of the criss-cross of tramlines in front of the dockyard gates, I stopped at the kerb and let the frame slide from under me; I was only twenty-seven but I had already given up swinging my leg over the saddle. "Leave the cursed things at home," mocked a housewife with bottles and bags and a wire-haired puppy on a length of string. I didn't know if she meant the bike or the trilby that I was trying to keep on my head. The street seller in his cloth cap and second-hand waistcoat bid me a good afternoon; he agreed that the weather would get worse. He was too weary to suggest that I needed one of the horse-hair brushes that were piled in a suitcase at his side. I walked past the remnants of old theatre posters on a wooden fence. The Hippodrome, Theatre Royal, Palais de Dance. Someone had pasted a brown paper banner across the display: 'Keep Warmongers Out!'

I left the bike with the dockyard specials, jaywalked between two opposing trams; then I was between the backs of the terraced slums. The smell of a broken sewer came up through the mud of the unmade alley. It got in my mouth – that smell – and I worked my tongue around, trying to get rid of it. A boy without trousers, his finger in his mouth and dribble down his face, kept an eye on me. He was clever enough to take things in and not show it but still he called, "You a copper?" although I didn't catch the words at a first try. The lad was barefoot and dirty; he wore a cut-down of his father's shirt. A swelling high up on his left cheek made me think that he had an abscess beneath the skin.

Six months before, I had sworn to serve the city without fear or favour. Well, where was the bobby who wanted these people on his beat? This was the alley where a prostitute had been found murdered, three years ago, and the killer was never caught. I doubted that our police had given her wretched body the same attention that was being devoted to the death of a dean's clerk.

I found the privy with a blue square in a white diamond painted on the outside wall. (I learned later that it was shared by six families from four houses.) A rickety staircase leaned against the outside of the house. I looked up and saw a square trap door at the top. "You'll not get in it," the boy said quietly. "Not until they want you, then you'll wish you'd never stopped to look." A vicar came out of a house further up the street and called him in.

I trod across a broken path and looked through the open back door.

Downstairs, they lived in one room. No-one could use the kitchen because the outside wall had fallen in, so they had boarded up the intervening door to keep out the worst of the cold. The main room, not thirteen feet square, was dark and damp and boxed in. The ceiling bowed alarmingly; not only couldn't a man stand up straight, but he couldn't see, from one corner, the top of a person sitting opposite. It was impossible to live here but three people did and sometimes this room was crowded with eight or ten. The air was cloying – your throat was never clear of it – and it was thick with heavy dust fallen out of the mixture that made up the walls, floor and ceiling. Long ago, they had lifted the tiles from the floor, just three or four remained on the dirt. They had filled in some of the holes with a sort of home made concrete. Slum-pattie, I learned to call it later. I could see how the roof beam was splintering along its length. (Really,

64

this bit of wood hadn't the strength to be called a beam at all.) I could hardly make out the figures because the room was thick with an orange cloud. I actually tried not to breath at first, then I kept each breath shallow and put a hand over my mouth when I talked.

The big man, made to look enormous in this room, laughed at me. "You'll not keep it out of your lungs, no matter what you do. It's in the log."

"I'm sorry," I coughed.

"Step in," he said.

He was standing against a wall, bent like a trailing plant over the toy fireplace. One lump of wood smoked; it was too wet in here for anything to burn properly. Because the fireplace had been made from bits of other things, most of the smoke wasn't drawn to the chimney but spread, like bad weather, across the room. The man coped with this atmosphere by smoking heavily from a stubby pipe. But the tobacco was unlike any that I had smelled before. I couldn't get rid of the notion that he was smoking some sort of dried dung.

A woman occupied the other half of the floor. She sat on a box with her old dress drawn up to her knees and her old legs stretched over a wooden tub of stale, soiled water. She took handfuls of fat from another, smaller, tub which she rubbed into her legs before soaking her hands and going back for more. I could see no health or beauty in it. She was doing it because she liked it, presenting a repugnant self-obsessed image, and I tried not to look at her. She didn't speak. She didn't stop what she was doing, showing far more than was decent in 1937, and she gave no hint that she picked up a word of what was said.

"You're done with," he said. He had a wild look about him; a fierce face made more warrior-like by menacing black centred eyes, piercing and messianic. He wore hobnailed boots and trousers that were caked, almost impregnated, with the sludge and soil of hard work. His arms were pitted with black scars and his cheeks were flecked with coal. He kept one thumb hooked in the belt loop of his trousers and picked at the other with two fingernails. That was all he had on one hand.

"I've been paid to shut you up," he said.

He spoke confidently, needing little slang and only occasionally reinforcing his words with shifts of his hands or shoulders. This man had not always been poor. But I was surprised by my reaction. He was stronger than me, very much so, and more practised at throwing people around, but from the first I wanted to fight him.

He shook his head. "You shouldn't have poked around the dead man's house. It wasn't your place to do that. But it was Annie Ankers' idea, no doubt."

I didn't answer.

"Let that be a lesson learned. Never do anything dear Annie says. She gets you into trouble."

"Her husband told you. He was listening."

"Just so. And very interested in you, he was. He'd been drinking with Big Elsie's sea captain so they were both very interested."

"And Soapy Berkeley?"

"Just Josh Ankers and the Captain. They were drinking alone. Your Ernest was in the room where the killing was done. You know that. But he has been questioned by Mr Gutterman and Mr Turncott so he's no concern of yours. Not any more. Do you see?"

The woman got to her feet and I made way so that she could carry the used water out to the lane. Immediately a dog barked at her. I heard her sit on the outside staircase. The house creaked and seemed to lean another couple of inches. Dust crumbled from the ceiling.

"Now, I'm going to stop you meddling."

"You don't frighten me," I said quickly.

He saw that I was amazed by my own bravado and he smiled. "I don't need to frighten you. You're already trapped. Let me tell you what you are going to do in a very few minutes. You will walk backwards from this room. When you turn around, you will see three men on the other side of the lane. A preacher, a marine and an old schoolmaster. They will see you climb up the stairs to my loft. Go carefully, please, because I don't live in a strong house. Of course, if anyone suggests that my witnesses are too convenient, I will produce countless others. These will be ordinary people but they will be believed because they will tell the truth. Not only will they see you climb the steps but they will hear what you do in the loft."

"You think you can force me up those steps?"

"What's in the loft?" he taunted. "Why, my Polly is. And she'll say that you violated her. She might even say that you're the father of her unborn child. All of it, true. All of it, Mr Machray, provable."

"That's outrageous!" I roared. "You keep a woman up there and force men on her?"

"No, you will walk willingly and Poll will be pleased to help. Believe me, in a very few minutes, you will. Now, if you stop asking questions about the murder of Hubert Wycherley, if you stop your bicycle rides, if you stop poking around houses that are no place for you to be – no-one will hear that you have been here. I've been paid to stop your nosing around. You are going to promise – oh, surely, you will – but don't you see that I need a guarantee. My Polly is my guarantee of your silence, your good behaviour."

"I want to see this girl. I want to see that she's all right."

"Oh my," he mocked. "Are you going to rescue her?"

"I want to see her," I insisted.

He went on laughing. "What are you going to try next?"

"This much," I said. "You talk like an educated man so ..." I was going to say 'listen to this' but that would have gone too far. "The people who have paid you are either murderers or traitors. Probably both. Murder is a small matter for you. I don't think you would be bothered about that. But I think you'll have nothing to do with treason."

He raised his eyebrows. "Indeed, I wouldn't. Not in these times."

"I'll agree to this. You want me to stop my questions. Well, I'll be more careful and if you need a guarantee of that, we'll come to an arrangement. In return..."

"In return, Mr Machray? Are you in a position to bargain?"

I dipped my head. "Because you'll have no truck with traitors. I want to speak to the man who runs dog fighting hereabouts and I think you're a man who can introduce me."

"I could do that. I could fix you up with Soldier Brock. But you are asking me to double-cross my paymasters. I will need a guarantee."

"Sir, you're too clever to be caught for murder but if your name is linked with treason, you'll swing."

"And you," he said ponderously, "will climb into my loft."

"I will," I said. "Because I want to see this poor girl. But I'll do her no harm."

* * *

67

She was lying on a hard bed of sack-cloths and tied-up bales. Daylight from little square window above the makeshift bolster made her face silver rather than fawn. The rest of her was brownie coloured. That was the only light there was. Her face was squashed in, with flat ears and awkward teeth and black gaps where there were none at the front. She was naked. A sack was drawn over her middle, covering the pit of her stomach and most of one leg. The other leg was bare to the top of her hip, telling tales of a thin and bony bottom. None of it – the bottom, the sacks, the squashed-in face and the tiny window panes – had been washed in weeks. My nose twitched as I trod across the dark floor.

"Be it the smell or the dust? Either ways can make you sneeze," she said, then teased, "I think it's the mites in air." She wasn't as old as me, but I couldn't really guess her age; she had been too badly used for that. She tried to hide something as I approached the bed. When I didn't try to look, she let me see the withered arm beneath the sacks.

"We're supposed to do something," she said. She tossed her head so that her curly brown hair fell back from her neck. "M'Da'll be waiting at the bottom of the staircase," she said. "He'll know if we don't. And Ma, she'll be listening through the hearth so you be careful what you say." She pulled at my shirt. "He'll be wanting you to give me a good doing-to, so that he'll be able to call on you. He wants to say, do as I say or I'll tell everyone what you did to my crippled daughter."

"You're not crippled," I said.

"I make do," she said. "I do with one hand what takes good girls two." She cocked her knee so that the sack fell away, exposing her private parts. (She's learned all her manners from her mother, I thought.) "He'll want to hear you doing me. You're mental if you don't."

I sat on the bed and lifted her puny shoulders until she was sitting up. "Polly, I've come to take you away from this. It's wrong, what people are making you do."

"Don't be daft. I don't want to go away. This is where I am and I damned-darned-well good at what I do. You ask anyone's who's been up here."

"But you don't have to do this."

"Why would I want to do anything that I'm not as good at? You, you're being a dafto. Now, too much talking spoils things," she said. "Won't you be getting your trousers down?"

I put a finger on her lips so that she closed her mouth over the mixed up teeth. Then I got her to sit in a way that kept her hair over her shoulders. I kissed her, trying to make it as tender as she would allow. She had been taught to feel through my trousers with her good hand. I nudged her fingers away but, when I went on holding her, her hand came back. It was what she was supposed to do.

She didn't put up with my kisses for long. She pulled herself away from my mouth and asked, "Are you going to do me good and proper or not?"

"I can't," I said plainly.

That bothered her. "How old are you?"

"Twenty seven," I said. "But probably three or four years younger."

I got us to sit side by side on the bedstead.

"You're not going to start talking, are you? He won't have it. I told you Ma will hear down the chim-lee and she'll be out there, telling him. If you were doing me proper, you wouldn't be talking."

"I've always said that fat boys take longer to grow up. We take longer to get around to things and, when we find a pleasure, we spend more time enjoying it. We're an indulgent lot. I don't mean greedy; greed means wanting more suet dumpling. No, we don't want more because we've learned to make the most of each mouthful before moving on to our pudding. You see, I've always said that fat boys need to value their own company. After all, few kids would want to be known as our friends and it was the promise of spending hours on my own that drew me to lorry driving."

She giggled. "You're scared of me, aren't you? That's what this talking's about."

"I simply loved long journeys with no-one to talk to. I took to the occupation with a passion that almost became an obsession. Within a few weeks, I had come up ideas for making the trips more efficient. Oh boy, did that make me unpopular? I hadn't considered how people would feel about efficiency. Thinking of others doesn't come with being fat, I suppose."

69

"You're squirming like you've got crabs," she said. "Is that it? You've got crabs?"

"Girls?"

"Who mentioned girls?" she said. "Oh God, you don't do girls. Is that it? Is that it, as well as crabs?"

"Well, I did take some time to get around to them. I used to stop overnight with Mr and Mrs Clarke and their daughter seemed to take a shine to me. But one day, Mrs Clarke met me on the doorstep. She said that Bette was having a baby and, if I knew what was good for me .... Well, I could hardly see how it was my fault. Betty was old enough to be my mother and I only ever did what she wanted."

She lost patience. Her good hand went to my flies and she set about unbuttoning. She hadn't got far when she pulled back. "Christ! You have got crabs!"

I shook my head. "Very bad sores, that's all. I've been cycling."

She thought for a moment, then said, "Well, you'll have to do something horrible to me instead. He won't take nothing less. And he'll be up here in a minute. Don't think that he won't set the dog on us, 'cause he will. You and me both."

"Don't be stupid. I'm not going to hurt you. God, Polly, you're like a slave. Locked up here and made to do these things."

Downstairs, someone broke into a coughing fit. They tempered it by stamping their walking stick against the wall. The whole house shook. Dust fell from the cob ceiling. 'Da', who was still sitting on the bottom step of the outside staircase, cursed profanely.

"He'll lose his head," Polly warned. She was on her feet and fetching a rope's end from the corner of the roof. "Hurry," she said. "Truss me up like a cooked fowl."

I didn't know how I was supposed to do that.

"Please you've got to violate me."

It was a word she had learned years ago.

"I can't do that, Polly," I said.

"Then..." Her mind raced for other ideas. "Then we have one of two choices and I don't care which. Either you'll have to – have to – do me, even if I catch your sores. I don't care. Or we must pray together. I'll say that you were a little crazy and wanted to save my soul. Four years ago, Da made a man came up here on Christmas Eve and we did just that. We knelt at the bed and we prayed for my soul."

"Your father put up with that?"

"I'll say not. Da' murdered him. He murdered him for his impertinence, then Da' sent him away with the fishers to be dumped." By now she had buttoned up my trousers and ushered me to her bed. "Kneel down. Hands together. We've got to be side by side."

"But if your father murdered the last one?"

"But afterwards, he said he was wrong and shouldn't have. And our Ma made him promise that if he any else came to save my soul, why, Da' will let him off with just a scar. A bloody cross on his dickie will do plenty, our Ma said . And you must see Mother Dowell for your scabs, d'you listen to me?"

"But, Polly, you've just told me that your father has killed a man."

PART TWO

THE BLOOD ON THE WALLS

EIGHT

Annie's Question

I don't think Brock had ever been a soldier and, probably, he had never been on safari but he had the weathered skin, the dry sun-bleached hair and the bowed legs of a bush scout. An old irregular. Certainly, he had passed seventy and was full of siege and trespass yarns. And he still wore khaki shorts and leather boots buckled at his knees. He was standing at the sanded, second-hand counter of the Hoboken's public bar with one polished top cap on the brass foot rail and two hands cradling a quart of muddy coloured beer. He had the place to himself because it was an hour before opening; the morning steward kept an eye from a nook between two doors and we heard Annie Ankers cleaning the back rooms.

"You were there!" he declared when I was still a dozen paces from him. "I know you were there!"

I thought he was talking about Polly's attic but I was wrong.

"I heard you talking with that rather pretty girl from Broadways three weeks ago."

"Three weeks ago?" I queried. "A pretty girl from Broadways?"

"For sure, fruit, though I think you lost her half way." He laughed. He had the pale blue eyes of an outdoor man. "My word! Half way! Half way, that's between Shap and Carlisle, I suppose. But I heard you tell her, no doubt about it, that you were on the Ten-Fifty-Four."

I smiled – a smug smile, I'm afraid – but I said nothing. He bought me a beer and I took a good mouthful.

"I've got to say, fruit, it's not the best way to lead a girl on. They'll probably debunk at platform three while you're still in the diner. I say, 27 April 1928."

"I think it was a Friday." I didn't tell him that I could remember the date with no trouble. I still had my copy of the morning paper with the Langdale and Bassett signatures across the headline. "I was only eighteen so it was all a bit of a thrill."

"It would be to any man with blood in his veins." He called to the barman and said that he'd buy me another drink. I wasn't half way down my first one. "Will you tell me about it?" he said.

"There isn't much to tell. You see, the company hadn't announced that it was 'on'. The staff were very excited but even they kept it quiet. At least, until we'd left Euston."

"But you must have known. The trains were split from the start."

"Well, yes. There was that." I took a dollop of beer.

"Yes, yes." He tapped his knuckle on the counter and eagerly took up my story. "Friday 27 April 1928. The LNER had advertised that they would run the Flying Scotsman on the following Tuesday. Now, the LMS, in secret, were determined that their own Royal Scot would steal the thunder. To do it first. To do it better. Because their route was longer, they'd make sure that LNER were neither the first nor the longer. That's why they had to run two trains that day. They couldn't stop at Carlisle or Symington, you see. It had to be non-stop. When did you know it was 'on' for sure?"

"I was travelling first class with a literary lady. She knew it before me."

"First class?"

I nodded. "I had to carry an important package for Owen and Owen and first class was thought to be the safest way."

"A literary lady?" He had to say it slowly to get the words out.

"A writer, I think. She was in the compartment before I climbed aboard. She seemed well up on trains. She said that the best detective novel would be a murder on a train when every one of the passengers had a hand in it, but it would need to be a non-stopper. Then she looked out of the window and said, 'Like this one, do you think?' I was very impressed. I was only eighteen and had a writer to myself for eight hours."

"Too late," he sighed. "It's already been done. Murder on the Orient Express. My niece gave it to me for Christmas, three years ago. She knows I like trains, you see."

"Ah, yes," I argued. "But not then. It hadn't been done then. Not on --- " and we cried out the date together " – 27 April 1928!"

"But no, no," he objected. "You knew before you spoke to your writing lady. You told our pretty girl from Broadways that you bought a morning a paper so that the crew could autograph it."

"Well, yes," I conceded. "I'd had word. Word got round actually. You know how it happens."

"So, the thrill. Tell me about the thrill."

I knew what he meant. Shooting through Carlisle without stopping to change crews and knowing for certain that it was on. They didn't stop to split the train at Symington – half going to Glasgow, half to the capital. No, they were going non-stop from London to Edinburgh for the first time and I was going to be part of it.

"Ah yes," I said. "Engine number 1054."

"And then, last year," he dreamed.

"Ah, yes," I agreed

Now, we shared the affinity of men who have the same images in their heads.

"The Princess Elizabeth. Euston to Edinburgh in just five hours, fifty three minutes and forty two seconds."

Then he slammed his beer glass down on the counter and glared at me. "The boss says I'm to tell you about dog fighting in our city. Is that right?"

"No, I want to know who runs the racket," I said.

"Ah, a dangerous question and never you mind the answer. You just listen to Brock's good advice. You want a dog that's not above twenty-five pounds in weight with grandparents a man can name, although you can't expect a pedigree that's written down. Never bother with a fawn or patch coat – no Birmingham colours, as they call them. You want a good black terrier, a proper Staffs-Bull with a head shaped like Annie's coal scuttle."

On cue, our Annie clanged two buckets together and swore out loud as she spilt dirty water across the flagstones of the back passageway.

"Most important, you want a dog that fights with no noise. No yelping or barking, nothing above a wet scowl."

"Where does the fighting take place?"

"You'll be told that when you've got yourself a dog. Men will want to deal with you, readily enough. When you take the rough whore in our dray yard, she doesn't need to call out her wares, does she?"

"Near the old Commodore's house on the cliffs?"

That interested him. "Never that old Brock's heard about and where's the sport that I don't know?" He fixed his old eyes on my face. "You worry me. You've heard of the Blue Cockatoo, sometimes called the Pink Cocktail or the Cockerel Club? Unlicensed dancing and drinking clubs. Always a little music from a four or five piece band. And Irish Dowell – yes, you've heard of her? The barmaid at this place, the Hoboken Arms. Well, she plays hostess at the Blue Cockatoo after hours." He laughed. "Her family don't like it. They don't like it at all!"

"I saw her walking down Goodladies Road," I found myself saying. I was picturing it. "She was wonderful, just wonderful."

"Well, her family don't like it. The Cockatoo is raided once a fortnight but it always opens next night in a new place. The Commodore you speak of, he puts up the money for these nightclubs, that's why the police never prosecute. But if he's moving into the dog fights, there'll be trouble. Dog fighting's not his business and he needs to learn his manners." Then he paused and weighed our conversation. "Tell me Mac, are you a troublemaker? Polly's Da' says you're too wise to cross him and silly Annie says you've got a soft heart. I guess I'd trust Annie's judgement because of her second sight. Nights in the veldt teach you to mark such things."

Then he told the barman to set drinks for Annie and me at a corner table. But when I stepped away from him, he called me back. "I can get you a good dog. It's come up just in the last couple of days and I'll offer you a third. But you must give me the money before tomorrow's dinner."

I didn't respond.

"A hundred pounds," he stipulated.

"I wouldn't know how to muster that sort of money," I said.

"No," he smiled. "I'm glad you said that. Any other answer would have called you a dishonest man."

78

Tiny Annie Ankers left her mop and bucket in the pub's kitchen and marched to the corner table. She beckoned me to join her but announced that she wouldn't do the job while the other men were listening.

We sat down together. "They want me to tell your fortune," she whispered. "You need to give me your hand."

Her fingers were light and would have given in to any resistance, but I let her stroke my palm and map the contours of my knuckles. After only a few seconds work, a mask seemed to fall across her face. She was wrinkled beyond her years; her bones were just not big enough to fill her skin, they left ripples where they bent. It was easy to think of Annie's limbs like branches on a tree with too much bark.

"There's something pulling," she said. "You want to be alone but you need other people."

I nearly said that she could have guessed that from talking with me but I didn't want to test her. I wanted to listen.

"He's told you, hasn't he?" she asked quietly. "He took me in for questioning. He has said that, Mr Gutterman, hasn't he?"

"He didn't 'take you in for questioning', Annie. He needed to write down what you saw and who told you what, that's all. You're not a suspect."

"Neither should I be, Mr Machray. I've always done my best, haven't I?"

"Everyone says, Annie."

"They've told you I'm old, haven't they? Well, I'm not. I'm the same age."

"I know, Annie. You told me. The same age as Elsie and Rose."

"And they still get men, don't they. Elsie's got her captain, hasn't she? And didn't Rosie spend time with our Mr Wycherley? So why can't I do it?"

"Do what, Annie?"

"Have a man apart from my husband?"

"Because you don't really want to."

"Anyway, Rosie was wasting her time because Hubert had eyes for another woman, younger than any of us."

I waited for her to explain.

79

"Young Irish, the girl who does nights in here. I saw them together a hour before he went to the Palfreyman."

I said, "You saw them at the staircase window, didn't you? I found her cocktail glass."

"It goes to show," she sighed.

I teased her. "What did Elsie say about that?"

"She said I was just a tell-tale. It was nothing to do with me and I was wicked for spreading gossip. How did you know I told her?"

"Oh, a lucky guess, that's all," I smiled.

"Well, anyway. It goes to show that everyone has a lover, so why can't I?"

"Because you're married, Annie. Rosie and Elsie are on their own. So was Hubert Wycherley. And Irish, too."

"But you're not," she said.

"Can you tell that from reading my hand?" I tried to move the conversation to other things. "Do they call you Canary because you're good at fortune telling?" I said.

"Nothing to do with it. I was Cannary before I married Joshua Ankers. Cannary's like Canary, isn't it. I was Annie Cannary at school, like my mother was before me. Mamma didn't have the sight herself but she always knew that I'd got given it from Grandma. Even when I was a babe, she knew."

"I see."

"Her name was Cannary too. My grandmother, if you can work it all out." She was kneading the flesh of my palm, twisting it to making the best of the light. "You have many children."

I wanted to ask, 'You mean I have already?' but the concentration on her face kept me quiet.

"It's because my grandma and mum didn't marry their lovers. That's why we're all Cannary."

She studied my hand again. "Ah, the love in your heart will never be fairly placed. You'll be a good shepherd." Then she shook her head irritably. "There, again. Always, I've got this vision of a man riding a horse across the range. He's like a cowboy, doing good."

"Yes, that could be like a policeman. A shepherd and a range rider. It could make sense, Annie."

I wanted to be helpful. I wanted to encourage her because here were a few moments when she could express something she was good at. But she shook her head. "He's forcing me to look at him. Ah, I have it!"

The others had come to our end of the counter and were looking over my shoulder. Did we all believe in Annie's strange talent? Well, no-one was turning their head away from it.

"Your greatest success will be catching the one who murders your true love. But your true love, no, she won't be the one you marry. Marriage comes later, much later, to a woman with a withered arm."

That seemed to break the spell. The steward and Brock went off laughing and Annie tried to toss my hand aside. "Go on," she said crossly. "Make of it what you will."

"I'll marry poor Polly," I persisted although it was plainly nonsense. "Do you know her?" I wouldn't let her release my hand. "She told me that her father had murdered a man in her loft."

"Oh, and don't worry about poor Polly's murder story. Polly's father made it up so that people would be frightened of him."

"You think I'll marry her?"

"But not while you're a policeman. Much later." She looked up and added kindly, "You'll make a good policeman. Real policemen, you see, don't understand. But you could."

There was an uneasy quiet.

"Understand what, Annie? What don't they understand?"

"Because they don't understand the real question. That's why the detectives are getting nowhere."

"The question?"

"Elsie will say it was Mrs Ritchers' old man, but don't let her. He was drinking with my Josh and the sea captain."

"What is the question, Annie?"

"Who shouted 'murder'?"

"Yes," I agreed with a relieved smile. "I asked that question on the first night and didn't get an answer. Mrs Ritchers was downstairs with Miss Ditchen. The mechanic was outside and came running in. Shaking Jacobs hadn't turned up at all and Soapy Berkeley jumped out of the window. So who came running down the stairs and shouted murder?"

* * *

81

In Harold Street, Elsie's judgement was prompt and straight to the point. "How obvious! Annie's such a clever girl when she puts her mind to it."

I was sitting on the top step of the staircase, watching as she dusted her trinkets on ledges. "Rosie and Mrs Ritchers. Michael, Soapy and poor Shaky. They are all accounted for. So, there must have been someone else in the room."

Then she put her cloth down and said disappointedly, "John Ritchers, of course. The landlord of the Palfreyman."

But Annie had already prepared me for that. "No, you see, he was drinking with Josh Ankers and your captain."

"Oh, was he now?"

"Annie says so."

"She says so, does she? So there must have been someone else in the house and that person is the murderer. Yes, as plain as the nose on my face." She stood up straight, put her hands on her hips and declared: "Talking of nosiness and what's on show. I'd be grateful if you would stop making out the shape of my underwear whenever I lean forward. You've been doing it for days and, 'though ten years ago I might have been flattered, I'm afraid it's rather distasteful when the admirer is a good deal younger than the trophy desired."

"I'm sorry. I ..."

"You didn't realise you were doing it? Poppycock. You've had the look of a rather grubby little boy who makes rude drawings in class."

I went red. "I'm rather ashamed, Elsie"

"Yes, well." She went to the back bedroom and carried on cleaning. I wanted to apologise properly, so I pulled myself to my feet and followed her, knocking politely on the door.

"You need to visit the Palfreyman again," she said without looking at me. With a great display, she stripped the bed and began to reverse the sheets. When I offered to help, she acquiesced without speaking.

"Elsie, I really am very sorry. I didn't think you'd notice."

As we 'shook the bugs from the blankets', I looked at the sun scorched walnut surface of her bedside table. The faded patches and dusty rims said that things had been re-arranged; perhaps there had once been a picture of a sea captain here, but he was gone now.

"You need to check that landing and work out where everybody was standing. Someone must have seen that man running down the stairs but no-one is telling."

"Elsie, can we talk?"

"Not about you," she said as she worked. "No we can't."

"No, about the other women?"

She sighed, almost angry rather than cross. "Do you know, you really need to cool down."

"No, Elsie. I don't mean like that. I mean about the murder. You told me that Rosie could kill someone if it was the right thing to do."

"For the sake of justice, I said, and I said that I was a bully."

"And that Annie would own up afterwards."

She puffed up a pillow. "I think we were playing, weren't we? I was saying silly things."

"I like puffed up pillows," I said.

"Yes, well. We've had enough talk like that. You'll be late for work. It's gone one o'clock. Get changed."

"So what about Mother Dowell and Irish?"

Elsie threw back her head and laughed aloud. "Oh yes! The Dowell women would murder because they could get away with it."

NINE

A Clinic of Peculiars

Irish Dowell's mother lived alone in a terraced house in a street with holes. Three years ago, workmen had dug up the pavement but couldn't put it back because the drains were broken. The drains must still be broken because no-one came to fix them, or to repair the pavement. At first, each of the three holes had a makeshift wooden fence. The mums and dads said that these could be taken down and used for cricket and rounders. Everyone thought this would show the council what for.

The widow had a large family – she was one of seven children herself and had brought a further seven into the world – so grandchildren, sisters, nieces, nephews and grown up children were always dropping round. But they never stayed over. Mother made sure that she had only one bed in her house and she slept alone.

The men who called on Mother Dowell came quietly. Along a back twitchel and through an open yard to her back door. She didn't need to ask what her visitors wanted; men came to Mother Dowell for only one reason. Often they found her on the step with her smock drawn up to bare her knees and a mug of brown ale at her side. Especially on warm afternoons like this.

* * *

Thursday was my last shift before a weekend off, so the sergeant brought me on duty at two in the afternoon and asked me to work until ten. He didn't say that I was one more policeman than he needed on nights, but I guessed as much. During that first part of my

84

patrol, the shops were open, children were running about and the roads were too full of traffic. I wandered away from my beat, looking to smoke my pipe in a peaceful spot, and found myself in the street where she lived. I went around the back because I wanted a look at the place without being seen.

"Ah yes," she cried, waving from the step. "Polly said you'd come. You want some brown beer with me, and a chat maybe. Nothing more, eh? Just a little listen." She screwed up her nose. "You and me."

She drew me into her kitchen. I took off my helmet and laid it on the draining board. Already, she was sitting the old kettle on the gas. "Go through, why don't you, and undo your tie. There's a nice chair in the parlour."

"A cup of tea on the step would be very welcome, Mrs Dowell," I said. I reminded myself that I was supposed to be walking up Goodladies Road, not resting in a lady's parlour.

She gave me a critical look. "Have you read Doctor Horrop?"

"Doctor Horrop?"

"For weight reduction, he recommends a milk and bananas diet."

"Eat bananas all day?" I chuckled. "Where would I get that many? Besides, Elsie decides what I eat. She does all the meals."

"Yes. We need to talk about you at Elsie's. But, first things first. Why don't you go through to the parlour," she insisted. "Both Polly and Soapy Berkeley have spoken to me about you. Really, I'm sure it would take just a minute to sort you out."

I collected my helmet. "Well, I'm on duty, as you can see, so perhaps another day."

I was half way out the door before she ushered me back in. "Remember, you need to prepare the milk carefully. Now, go through and sit down." She watched me walk into the front room, giving me no chance of escape this time. "Allow a quart bottle to stand overnight," she continued. "Then pour off the top quarter."

"The skim," I said. I sat in her armchair and opened my knees so that my helmet could sit between them. The parlour was small and had a heavy oak table in the middle. Mother Dowell had draped a white sheet over it. I saw some old stains but it looked well washed and clean enough. A fashionable fox fur was hanging on the back of the door. It had purple beads where its eyes should have been; I wondered if she had skinned it herself.

She shouted from the kitchen, "You have taken your hat off, haven't you?"

I said that I had.

"Good. That means you've settled to stay for a few minutes. Now, where did we get to? Oh, yes the skim. He recommends four good tumblers of skim milk and you should eat six large ripe bananas each day. Choose them with little brown freckles on their skins. Those are the fully ripe type."

When I said, "Really, I don't need to lose weight that much," she poked her head into the room. She put her face down and raised her eyes to give me that look of a disappointed teacher. She said, "I think we'd do better with our trousers off, don't you?"

I sat, open mouthed.

"I've been picturing it for several days," she said. The kettle whistled and Mrs Dowell went off to make a pot of tea. She allowed a minute or two, then called through, "It's better, dear, if you take everything off, socks and all." The next time I saw her, she was stirring something black and horrible in a shaving mug. She screwed up her nose again, "Less messy, like that. Do you know what I've been picturing?"

I said that I didn't.

"I said that I'd been picturing it for days. Do you know what it is?"

"Really, I can't guess."

"Both my sons will go off to fight and before the war's over, my young daughter will be running a pub on her own. Now, can you just picture that?"

I tried to say that she shouldn't worry; I doubted if there would be war, this year or next.

"Can you imagine that? No, my lads will come back and find their little sister – the same little one they've shielded and protected, fought for, no less, for years – in charge. That's it, you see. The one who runs the pub in our family always sits at the head of the dinner table. It's always been the same. Don't call her Irish, I think that's so unfair when Iris is a really pretty name."

86

"Yes, she is very pretty," I said.

She chuckled. "You must ask her about Rosie and Elsie. She has the very best story about those two. Constable Machray, you'll be well rid of them, both of them. A couple of cross women, they are, and Annie – just as wicked, just as vengeful – she runs between them like a hungry cat."

"What does your daughter know, Mrs Dowell?"

"Oh, just picture the boys' faces, seeing their little sister in charge. He's very popular in America, you know."

"Doctor What's-his-name?"

"Horrop. He's quoted in a new book called Weight Reduction Diets and Dishes. I'll make sure that Iris has a copy in the Hoboken's kitchen."

"I've told you," I insisted. "I lodge with Big Elsie."

"Yes. And it's time you moved out."

"I don't see why. And besides, I couldn't move into the Hoboken because the Chief Constable would never allow a recruit to lodge in a public house."

"I'm sure that he doesn't allow constables to catch VD but that hasn't stopped you."

"What! No, it can't be! It's rough cycling that's all!"

"Have you been in Elsie's bed?" she asked. "Is that where you got it?"

I told her that Elsie and I hadn't been intimate in any way. "I call in for warm muffins at night, that's all."

"She says you watch the shape of her bottom. She says that you wait at the bottom of the stairs and watch her go up."

"That's not fair!" I cried.

"Don't worry about the Chief Constable. I'll have a word with your nice Sergeant Martindale. Be ready to move out in the morning. Now look, you haven't stirred from that armchair and we need to get a move on. We've caught this little bother nice and early. We should be able to scourge you of your sins with very little trouble. Now, I'm going back into the kitchen where I shall count to twenty and when I come back .... face up on the table and legs wide apart, d'you hear?"

"Look," I croaked meekly. "I'm just a bit sore from cycling. It'll be fine."

"Yes, very likely it will. Just think of it as all those young women getting their own back." Again, she went back to the kitchen. Then in a bizarre comedy, this broad girdled hick doctor in a pinnie and heavy soled brown shoes tried to sing the lyrics from her new 78. 'Oh They're Tough, Mighty Tough in the West.' When she sang that men shouldn't be lilies, she was talking about me. And when she said that their triggers needed to faster than the rest, it hurt. She was out of tune and made up the words when she forgot. But the spirit wasn't lost. Brave cowboys don't cry and neither should policemen without their trousers. She carried on for three minutes, each verse mocking me more than the last.

"She saw Rosie robbing a sailor," she said as she came back to the room.

"Who?"

Slurp, slurp, slurp went the shaving brush in the mug.

"My Iris did. Didn't I say she knew the best secrets about those two." She looked at me. "You might find it more comfortable with your hands behind your head. Now you haven't moved an inch and I'm counting down from twenty."

A lump of cheap coal cracked in the grate and the gas dimmed in the mantles for a second or two. I got to my feet. I gazed at a framed print that was looking down from the wall. An engraving of George Romney's 'Girl Reading'; she looked very peaceful and fulfilled, but I would have preferred her not to be there.

* * *

Two hours later I was off duty but I was no longer welcome at Elsie's and no room had been fixed at the Hoboken Arms, so I walked the streets that night. I tried to keep out of sight because I was still in uniform and that was against the rules. I dawdled through the crooked lanes and tight passages to the dirty old quay. The little harbour was empty of fishing boats. Just half a dozen rowing boats, used by the waterman for going to and fro, were tied up at the opposite wall. Every now and then they would be caught in a ripple of water and jostled together. (An old ferryman was sleeping in one of these boats but I didn't see him until much later.) The night had closed in and I was sure that no-one else knew I was there, standing at the quayside, gazing into the muddy water. Then the woman from the waterman's pub waddled across the broken ground and put a mug of beer on the bollard beside me. "Put your change away," she said as I felt through my pockets. "I want to thank you for doing the right thing by Bertie without tearing the rest of us apart. You're looking for the truth by going quietly down the streets and round the houses." She growled, clearing her tubes I supposed, and her flesh shook; she had a fat neck like a great wodge of undercooked suet. "That's important to us," she said, recovering herself. "You're just the sort of copper we need in these parts."

"It doesn't feel like that. I don't think I'm much good at all. I'm not cut out to be a policeman."

"Won't you come indoors with me and we can play gramophone records until dawn."

I didn't know what to make of her suggestion.

"I have a regular called Jamie," she said. "He's very sweet and brings us very American records from, hmm, America."

But the landlady seemed to be a rather unpromising lady with whom to listen until dawn. So, I said no. I'd stay at the water's edge, I said. Thank you very much.

She grunted and went back into the pub but she was soon out again. She carried a Victor gramophone to the table outside the front door. She wound it up and got a dance record going. She left the lid open so that the guitar music had a lively crisp tone. She put two empty wine bottles on the table, each had a candle in its neck and she lit them, scorching her fingertips when the match burned too close.

I stepped back from the water's edge. "This town's run by the ladies who run the pubs," I observed.

"We try not to tell people." Reflections of candlelight flickered across her sow-like face. "Aren't the best families where mother wears the trousers?"

"Who's the music?"

She leaned over the gramophone and tried to read the label as it raced round, 78 times a minute. Her eyes couldn't make such movements on their own and had to take her head with them, producing a wobbling and nodding on her collar of suet.

"Blind Willie Dunn," she said.

"It sounds like two guitarists."

"Or one playing very quickly. I'll ask Jamie."

The landlady's daughter was about my age. She came out and told us off for playing the music too loud. She said we'd wake her father and they'd never get him back to sleep again. She was smoking a cigarette through a silly looking holder and had paste jewellery on a necklace that joggled as far down as her tummy button. She started to dance by herself; sometimes she wandered twenty or thirty years from her mother and me.

A burley character with wet trousers and dripping boots emerged from the steps that reached down to the water. I didn't see any boat that he could have come from.

"Got James's records out again, have you Missus?" he chuckled. He was chewing tobacco and looked ready to spit it out.

A couple of other people appeared. One of them, a long armed youth in stretched braces, danced with the daughter. I thought that a party might get going and I was nervous of being in uniform. But they were a half hearted lot. Just as I was. I kept apart from them and went to look down at the water again. Then, everyone else had gone and the landlady and I were alone.

"It's lovely, isn't it. Sometimes I sit out here with just the lights from the boats to look at and I think that nothing can be wrong, anywhere in the world. The harbour, it's so peaceful that it makes you believe that there can be no trouble, no war, no more murders. Listen ..."

I looked at her, then shook my head. I didn't know what I was listening for.

"You've been standing on your own for half an hour and you've not noticed?"

"No. I don't think I've noticed anything."

"Nothing you haven't heard?"

"Not really."

"The cathedral clock hasn't chimed since Monday midnight," she said.

TEN

The Detective Goes to Bed

The detective separated his jacket from the coat hanger and laid both on the counterpane. He slipped off his waistcoat, stretching his shoulders before he fitted it over the hanger. He patted it, as if to remove any dust. Then, having checked that the key to his London office was in his wallet and the wallet was safe in the jacket's inside pocket, he put the jacket on top of the waistcoat and returned everything to the wardrobe.

He coughed neatly.

He took off his elastic shirt-bands and placed them on the bedside cabinet. He kept these to hand because they were so easily lost in the mornings. He whistled lightly as he removed his Stratton cuff links. ('Cuff Link Comfort for Busy Men.') Then he unknotted his tie and removed his detachable collar, dropping the stud and the cufflinks into the middle of the shirt-bands. He collected the face towel and wash bag from the hook behind the door and poured water from the china pitcher to the bowl on the washstand. Both the pitcher and the bowl were decorated with pictures of flowers.

Chief Inspector Eustace Turncott liked to pretend that he was well behaved when he stayed away from home. Keeping a tidy room and undressing in an orderly manner was part of that.

At twenty past ten, he presented a sober and conservative figure – a right thinking gentleman – sitting upright in bed with puffed up pillows supporting his back. His pyjamas jacket was buttoned to the top, his spectacles sat squarely on his nose and his knees made a very neat shape beneath the blankets. He had been careful not to ruffle the counterpane. His Christie for Christmas remained on the bedside cabinet. Turncott was reading a library copy of Island of Sheep, the novel that Sergeant Willis had recommended because of the car chase. He was looking forward to that chapter but, playing by the rules, he would not skip any of the preceding pages.

The bedroom was square, cold and unhomely with faded floral wallpaper and furniture that had been brought from other parts of the house. Rosie Ditchen had promised to light some coals in the empty grate but Eustace didn't expect to see them. However, he had worked out that, by wrapping up and being in bed, he could be cosy in the little room, so he had closed the frail curtains (so shoddy that they almost gave way in his hands), turned off the ceiling light and relied on the bedside lamp that flickered because of a loose connection.

When Rosie climbed the stairs with cocoa on a tray and a packet of cigarettes in the vee of her dress, she was repeating in her head, 'Tempt him. Confuse him. He won't know whose side he's on.' He had left the door ajar so that Rosie had only to lean on it gently.

"I'm giving you two of Elsie's homemade oat biscuits. Made just Monday and allowed three days to air." She put the tray on the crowded dressing table, turned to face him and said, "I'll open the curtains and we'll manage by the streetlight." Without waiting for a reply, she stooped to unplug the lamp, then stepped through the dark to the window.

She was right; the light from the street was quite enough. Eustace heard horses in the barrack's yard. Someone was whistling on their way home from the pub. A giggle, and a woman ran across the street. Now Rosie stepped out of her dress and stood in her shoes and socks and her underwear. Eustace thought, Good Lord, she looks much bigger than she did in her clothes. He was surprised by the bumps and ripples that ruffled her petticoat. She walked to the end of the bed, a little to one side where she knew her reflection would be caught in the dressing table mirror. She had kept her hair in its bun; light from the streetlamp seemed to emphasise her emerging grey. Satisfied that the gentleman in his bed could see both sides of her, she untied the laces at the front of the petticoat and pushed it down until it was a skirt on her hips. The brassiere was boned and chunkily made and didn't tantalise. She turned around and Eustace saw that the catch had been broken and had been mended with a pink ribbon that the woman could release by pulling at one strand. Rosie, who had practised this in her head many times, was sure that, before tomorrow, the man would be eager to do whatever she asked. She hated him; but hadn't she learned to use her body against the men she despised? She'd done it twice before and each time she had won.

'Tempt him. Confuse him.' She waited for unnecessary seconds to pass, then she untied the garment and kept turning around so that she was facing him again when her funny shaped breasts fell free.

'They don't move,' he thought as she clambered onto the bed. She twisted and bent like an ungainly schoolgirl, no good in a PT class. They were small and firm but, in Turncott's words, each had a solid full-bodied undercarriage with an underdeveloped superstructure so that the snouts peaked like turned-up noses. 'I call them my puppies,' she whispered, but Turncott pictured two flat tyres on a sidecar.

Then, just as he decided that he'd prefer her not to, she tucked her thumbs in the elastic of her pants (surprisingly lacy for a straight-laced bird like Miss Rosemary Ditchen) and pulled them down. She covered herself quickly but he managed a glimpse of her secrets. Lordie, Lord. Surely not – but surely, wasn't that the best nest he'd ever been close to. Neat and thick and a rich ginger colour. He almost found the gumption to ask for a better look.

"We'll see," she said, reading his mind as she pulled the blankets up to her shoulders.

Got him, she thought. Got him.

But Turncott's face had changed. 'We'll see' was a phrase from people in charge and, from that moment, he resolved not to like her.

"Oh dear, oh dear. Never mind," she sighed, her hands having explored things beneath the sheets. "We'll soon flurry you up." As she came close to him, his nose twitched at her curious smell. She had the flavour of cooking oil that the Mediterraneans use in London. Maybe that's what nourished her nest so well. Now, they were holding each other and Rosie was pushing different bits of herself into the tucks and corners of his body. When he didn't respond, she enquired, "Would you like me to whisper a story?" But the deflated Chief Inspector couldn't suggest a tale to tell.

Face to face and so entwined that not kissing produced an

uncomfortable self consciousness; it wasn't going well. Rosie felt the first moments of doubt; she had cast the bait across the waters but the trout had no appetite.

She had brought him this far and she was determined to finish the job. 'Tempt him. Confuse him. He won't know whose side he's on.' That evening she had allowed him to spot where she had hidden Wycherley's papers; she had hinted that she was working for someone but not their old captain, Buttermilk Dolby; she had even opened up the question that her secret endeavours might be for sale.

"Oh dear," she said again. "Oh dear." Then, "I bet,' and she turned over and pushed her rump against him. At last, she sensed his body answer. When she swooned with phoney exhilaration and he rolled towards her, she pushed harder. Then she sang quietly, 'Wasn't that a dainty dish to set before the king,' and spoilt it for him.

They sat up and smoked. For twenty minutes, they didn't talk. And because she didn't leave and he didn't tell her to go, an unspoken acceptance emerged that Miss Ditchen and Mr Turncott were going to manage the encounter, somehow.

Rosie slipped from the sheets and, allowing herself to stay naked, stepped across the cold carpet to the open curtains. The street below was empty, but they could hear traffic elsewhere in the city. Standing aside from the window, she lit a cigarette. Then, once it was going properly, she laid it carefully on the window sill while she freed her hair to fall half way down her back. It was coarse, but neither dry nor brittle and it was much longer than Turncott expected. He thought, what a waste, keeping it in a bun like that. Rosie collected the cigarette and stood with one arm under her breasts, the hand supporting the elbow of the other arm. She smoked. She turned, just a little, to make sure that he still needed to look long and hard to see her as he wanted to.

Got him.

She stood and kept quiet and let the night time do its work. Once or twice, he moved in the bed but gave no clue that he was interested in joining her. Still, she knew that he was watching. Studying her. Trying hard. She finished the cigarette and, using the excuse that she had no ashtray, she opened the window and threw the stub out. She leaned forward – her elbows on the outside ledge but her breasts safely covered – and offered her bare bottom to the Chief Inspector.

The night had the feel and tincture of graphite – a roughness which, Rosie knew, would make her smoke too many cigarettes. All the other households had gone to bed and the road was empty of traffic. She looked for any lonely figure strolling along the pavements but no-one was out tonight. A strong amber light from the Customs House loft crossed the street in a hurried sweep, as if it came from a rotating beacon. It was an unusual reflection and, as Rosie stood at the bedroom window, she tried to work out what obstruction could be causing the phenomenon. Then she wondered if the light was coming from a ship at sea. No. No, that was nonsense. But before she could solve the puzzle – could it be from a neon sign? No, that idea was just as silly – she spotted a figure in the doorway opposite. A young man in an open raincoat. He was illuminated for only a few seconds and Rosie could count to eight between each sweep of the lamp. She heard Turncott climb out of the bed and everything in her wanted to turn and face him; she was, after all, still bare and needing him to make love to her.

That's when he came to her and, as he tampered with her body, she said carefully and softly, "As good as doing it in the open air."

When he stepped back from her and left her at the window and leaned his shoulders against the wallpaper, just a couple of feet away, he said, "You were excited."

"You bet."

"I mean, while the youth was being caned in the night. I think you were excited. You told it all like a tragic tale but you had a sparkle in your eyes. And you are not, Rosie Ditchen, a lady who sparkles, ordinarily. I'll tell you what I think. I think you were just eighteen, lying alone in your bed in a big school house and listening to the toll of the bell. You could picture all the preparations. Then the bell stopped and, I say, your excitement was overwhelming at that point. You see, Miss Rosemary Ditchen, that's what makes you the sort of pussy cat that eats a vole after dark and spits out bits of its tummy."

"That's horrible." She had moved to the dressing table. Now, she came forward and began to search for her dress among the discarded clothes.

"You were right," he said.

"I was?"

95

"When you said that Buttermilk Dolby suggested I should lodge with you."

"No. No, I don't work for him anymore." She tried to get the dress around her but it wouldn't tie up. Quickly, she gathered up the rest of the garments.

"You were his agent," he argued.

No, she thought. This was wrong. "He makes people do what they don't want to do. He's a puppet-master."

"He wanted to know what Hubert Wycherley was up to. That's why he commissioned you."

"I told you. I don't work for Dolby anymore."

"Then who do you work for? The Commodore? Is that it?"

"I'm going downstairs," said Rosie Ditchen.

"All of it, Rosie. I need to know all of it."

She stared at him and said, "I realise now. The man in the doorway."

"The man across the street. Is that who you mean, Rosie? Put the clothes down, Rosie. You can't run away."

She nodded and went back to the window. The bundle of clothes fell away from her. "He's got the file from my sitting-room. He's stolen it."

Turncott was standing behind her, his breath disturbing her hair. She turned away from the window. 'You've double crossed me,' she wanted to say but nothing came out. For the next five long, aching minutes this woman wouldn't utter a word. Turncott was standing, naked and stringy, limp and as frightened as she was – holding a knife in his hand. Her face said that she understood everything and Turncott couldn't tolerate that. He raised the dagger high in the air, fixed his eye on the pulse in her neck and lunged down at her.

Rosie dropped to the floor. The man stumbled, followed her down, then let go of a horrid, squawking, gurgling, neighing sound as his own weight stuck the steel blade in his chest. His blood hit the floor. It splattered the far wall and, when a back spasm kicked out his legs for a last time, the blood spurted across the ceiling, leaving a gruesome trail from one picture rail to another.

Rosie, uninjured, got to her knees. Her hands were soaked with his blood and she smeared it over her face and down the front of her body without realising what she was doing. She scrambled away from the corpse, the floor hurting her knees, her fingers in her mouth, her toes tightly curled.

The body by the window seem to grow whiter with each second. A cold white – porky and smelling gone off. It was impossible not to think of dead meat.

Rosie stared. They were both naked, both dirty with blood and both on the cold floor. She had the ridiculous sense that they were children whose naughty play in the nursery had gone horribly wrong.

ELEVEN

Faggots in Dumplings

By one in the morning, I was looking for somewhere to sit in the warmth from the cathedral's boiler room. It was underneath the south annex and the heat came up through a hole in the church wall. A wooden bench fitted nicely in the draft but the verger thought that it attracted tramps at night so he removed it each morning. Religiously. That night, the back legs had been wedged between the stones of the war memorial rockery. I was working to dislodge them when a shrill cry of 'Murder!' turned my head.

A young boy in his dressing gown and slippers was running up the church path. His hands waved in the air and his yellow hair stood on end.

"Murder again! Murder, once and for all!"

The sight and sound of the fellow had a touch of pantomime. I stood in the middle of the path, held my arms up and went 'Whoa!' as you might do to a horse.

"There's been a murder, Mister. At Number 83. Blood and guts everywhere, all over the floor. They'll be livers and kidneys and ..."

I interrupted in my best policeman's voice. "Well, partner, you had better show me." He started to skip ahead but I collected his little hand and advised, "Policemen never run, neither do their helpers."

For an instance, a stark image of Wycherley's brains filled my head. 'Pat-a-cake, pat-a-cake.' I drew breath and managed to keep the bile down.

"Now, what are you doing shouting murder in the middle of the night?"

"We're the neighbours above the wicker shop and we heard all the shouting. Enough to wake the dead, my mother said it was. She sent our Pop round and Pop said that Miss Ditchen had got as far as the porch and was covered in blood. 'No sight for a woman, Jean,' he said and told our Gilbert to run for the police. Except our Gilbert's never been quick enough and I was out of the house and gone before he had his boots on."

"I expect you'll be in trouble," I warned.

"Ordinarily, but people will be too busy to worry about that. Anyways, I'll say I was too scared to stay indoors."

"All that liver and kidneys," I said lightly.

He asked if I had ever seen intestines and that picture of Wycherley's brains snagged in my mind again.

* * *

It was four in the morning and no-one was ready for the horrid doings in Number 83 to be exposed to honest daylight. "No, no, Timothy, it was a lady undressed," said his mother, thinking, as she tried to tuck him in for two more hours, that her words were so much more decent that the 'bare woman' he preferred. Timothy used her term when he repeated the story from his bedroom window.

Already, the early merchants were going about their business. Sid's horse was pulling an empty cart to the top of George's Hill. And, down at the quay, a well fed matron in a blue and white smock was grumbling because she had so little to load onto her seafood barrow. "What was a lady doing up in Number 83?" she wanted to know. "And he wasn't from hereabouts neither. Sounds like a secret assassination to me."

Someone said, "You mean assignation," but the fat woman only replied, "Dukes and ladies, you ask me. Ask me, and I'll say there was more than just a couple."

Neither the Chief Constable nor the Commodore-in-Charge wanted people to hear about spies and traitors so they simply nodded when the dirty details of passionate murder grew further and further from the truth. In two hours, decent families would be dressed and taking breakfast. By then, the stories of bare bodies, bloodied in an

99

upstairs room would be shrouded in safely washed terms and worthy Christian doubt. 'Your mother and I are sure that people are exaggerating, you mustn't believe them. Besides, I'm sure that the gentleman was Miss Ditchen's brother, so they'd be in their pyjamas at least.'

Mrs Ritchers had opened the Palfreyman for the Commodore-in-Charge, the Chief and me. She put us at the table where Rosie Ditchen had sat on the night of the murder and assured us that no-one in the street would hear our conversation. "She's not been arrested, you say?"

"No, Mrs Ritchers. She's done nothing wrong and she's free to leave the police station at any time." The Chief suggested that three glasses of beer would be welcome. Then, when the landlady was behind the counter, he called, "Rosie will be sitting at her table this evening, I shouldn't wonder."

The Commodore's face expressed some doubt about that.

"You've showed that you're steady under fire, young Ned," said the Chief. "And you were right to ring Rosie's contact number, just as she told you, before you informed the station. I shall make sure all the sergeants understand. A reliable hand in a tight spot. I shall make it clear." He stayed with us while I repeated my story for the third time, then he went to fuss around Mrs Ritchers. If he was trying to flirt, well, he made a twerp of himself. He ended up working at the sink with a tea towel over his shoulder.

The Commodore watched these goings-on with some disdain and he had started his second pint of beer before he spoke properly to me. "We need to give your Chief an easy time on this. He retires at the end of the month. I'm making a presentation to him at the Guildhall and I wouldn't want any doubts about his abilities to spoil that."

I saw the smudge of blue paint on his index finger. I smiled. But this man wasn't to be made fun of. He was peculiar and eccentric but he wouldn't be ridiculed. When he cocked a quizzical eyebrow at me, I said simply, "A little mystery, solved."

"Great Scott, man!" The words flubbered on his chops like sticky jelly. "What else were you thinking?"

"You've painted a portrait of his favourite horse, haven't you? The one that he lost in the Boer War. You've painted it with his current wife standing beside it in her riding habit."

"An easy enough guess. Yes, yes."

"And she's been sitting for you at your house on the cliff?"

"Of course, of course. Goodness sakes, what else were you thinking?" he repeated. "You were clumsy in my back garden. We both saw you and quickly supposed what you were up to. I decided to keep you quiet by pushing you into the hands of the Blackamore Lane man. A word with an old man who uses Teggs' smokers shop was enough to bring you there. When I saw that the dirty bruiser couldn't intimidate you and you pressed on with your investigation – keeping outside of the police force, as much as you could – I realised that you were the sort of man we're going to need in the future. It's not that you managed to work on your own. The real matter is that you preferred to work that way. Perhaps, it's the only way you can work. Mr Machray, there's going to be a war. Not this Christmas, but we'll have taken up arms before Christmas '38. When that happens, I don't want you to volunteer. My office will make sure that others co-operate with your delay. Please, believe me, you can best serve your country in other ways."

He was so stuck up that he seemed to talk through his nose. I studied him, trying to work out how he did it, and my attention seemed to make him do it all the more. He kept his head back so that he gave the impression of looking over my shoulder when he spoke to me. At first, I thought he was keeping an eye on Mrs Ritchers and the Chief – they were muttering, head to head, at the counter. Then I wondered if the Commodore was so used to scanning horizons from the bridges of ships that he couldn't help taking a long view and had to look down on people close to him, as if he were peering through bifocals balanced uncertainly on his nose. That nose, again. It was very nasal. When he sniffed, it twitched irritably like a terrier sneezing.

"Hubert Wycherley discovered a weakness in our city's air defence," he said. "When he was murdered, Turncott took up the case with the intention of passing Wycherley's document to the enemy. Do you agree?"

"I can't say that, sir."

"Quite. To steal the file was too risky, so he decided on a little distraction. He convinced our Rosie to sleep in his bed and, while they were upstairs, Turncott's accomplice walked into the house and took the documents."

"That's what Rosie told me," I agreed.

"Do you believe her?"

"Well, sir. She doesn't look passionate."

"Passionate. How polite, Constable. But loose? Do you say that she's a loose woman?"

I avoided the question. "Other people know her better than I do," I said.

"In that case, let's go to the next step. Turncott realises that she's spotted the accomplice. The game is up; he tries to kill her but he falls on his own knife."

"Yes, sir. I agree."

"So Turncott is the villain. A spy and a traitor."

"This is all new to me, sir. I've never been involved in anything like this. Sir, I have to say that he tried to get me to recover Wycherley's papers. I said no."

The Commodore considered this. "So, he had to use one of his local burglars. Did you discuss Wycherley's murder with him?"

"I said, sir, that we should turn the evidence on its head."

He smiled. "Not even Nelson did that."

"At first, I thought that Wycherley had discovered evidence of dog fighting."

"Dog fighting? In the dell by my place, you mean? Turncott met me in the dockyard. He told me that a keen young copper thought I was running the sport. If I was up to something, he said, I'd do well to let it lie for a few months. Then, he said that fifty pounds would make sure nothing came of your suspicions. I didn't pay up, of course,"

"At first," I repeated nervously. "I thought that Wycherley wanted to disrupt the racket, tell the police about it, perhaps – but now, I think he wanted to join in. That's what I meant by turning the evidence on its head but Mr Turncott never asked me to explain. I think that Wycherley wanted to buy a dog."

The Commodore asked directly, "Who told you that?"

"Nobody. And I don't know it's true, of course. But a man in the Hoboken said that a dog was for sale. He didn't say that Wycherley had wanted to buy it, but he said that a sale had 'fallen through' on the day of the murder."

"Did he tell you –" The Commodore wondered, his hands brought up to his face in a parody of prayer. " – the dog owner's name?"

I shook my head.

"The owner's name was Rosie Ditchen."

Mrs Ritchers came from the kitchen with two dishes of faggots in dumplings. "You'll need these." She put the condiments on the table, and half a loaf of bread in thick slices, then she took a third dish to the Chief at the counter, leaving the Commodore and myself alone in the corner. "I know not one of you will have eaten properly since yesterday teatime," she said.

Yesterday teatime, I would have described Rosie Ditchen as a compact, dowdy woman, well past it, who kept her own counsel and dreamed only clean daydreams. But now, I couldn't avoid the evidence that she could be talked easily into a married man's bed and made her money by mixing with crooks and fighting dogs.

"A paid informer," said the Commodore. "Your first picture of her is the correct one. A forgettable woman who watched things quietly. There wasn't much going on in this part of the city that she didn't know about." He sipped at his beer. "That's why my department financed the Cockatoo nightclub. So that our agents could get close to the racketeers and scoundrels. But Rosie was too good for that tactic. She had to broaden her circle of friends and get in close. But no-one suggested the fighting dogs; it was her own idea. Strangely enough, people could believe it of her – she was quiet, full of sense and had a naughty edge to her. She was always threatening to tell tales. Very clever, I thought, the way she did that. When I heard what she was up to, I arranged for the pit to be dug on the cliffs, but your Chief wouldn't tolerate that. He said that he could keep an eye on the dog fights in Bunyard Lane. That's where he wanted them to stay."

"So your pit was never used?"

He shook his head and carried on eating.

"There's a thread to all this, sir, if we want to follow it.

"Yes, yes," he said with his mouth full. "Please."

"Wycherley surveyed the air defences along the coast near your home and found a dog fighting pit. He was fascinated by it and made an offer to buy Rosie's dog. Now, if that purchase had gone ahead, Rosie would have had enough money to 'put things right'.

The Commodore frowned. "What things?"

"I don't know," I conceded uncomfortably. "But it's what every one has said to me. 'Give Rosie chance to put things right.' I can't make any more sense of it."

"Come on, man. Who's your suspect? Who killed Bertie Wycherley?"

"The women who have gathered around this murder have been telling tales on one another. It's as if, collectively, they know that one of them is guilty but they can't agree which. Take Elsie, my landlady …"

"Yes, yes. Big Elsie. But why on earth should she kill Wycherley?"

"No, sir. I don't think she did, but I was going to tell you what she said."

"Ah, I shouldn't have interrupted. Go ahead."

"She says Rosie would kill a man for the sake of justice, Annie Ankers would always own up to the crime and Mrs Dowell and her daughter would only do it if they could get away with it."

I tore a slice of bread in two and waited for the Commodore to dunk first. He saw that I was hesitating so he obligingly dipped a crust into the faggot gravy. "And what about your Elsie?"

"She's not really 'my Elsie', sir. It's just that I lodge with her."

"Quite, but what does she say about herself?"

"She agrees she's a bully."

"Ah," he said, nodding as he pressed a crust of dumpling to his fork. "She's the wicked one, is she?" He dusted more pepper onto the faggots. "Well, we have to play cherry stones, don't we?"

I laughed. "When I thought of that last night, I ended up with an awkward question."

"Come on, then. Rich man, poor man, beggar man, thief."

"Rich man, first?"

"That's the Dowells," he said.

"And Annie Ankers is the poor man, I agree, but that leaves Rosie and Elsie for the beggar man and the thief."

104

He thought for a moment. "Rosie's the beggar man."

"That what's I thought, so Elsie is the thief."

"Good Lord, Machray. Your Elsie ends up as a wicked bully and a thief."

I shook my head. "But that doesn't make her a murderer."

"No, no. We can't hang people because they're the wrong sort."

I asked, "Which one of them would want to murder me?"

"Great Scott, do you feel at risk? Is anyone following you?"

"Not that I've noticed."

"Then what makes you ask?"

"Well, suppose that Wycherley had followed the same trail that I've found. He would have found your house on the cliff and the pit dug for dog fighting. I've no doubt that he was warned off by the thug in Blackamore's Lane; probably, he had found poor Polly in the loft. But what had he done then? Something that had led to his murder? You see, I think that I've poked the same wasp's nest that he disturbed. So a good reason to kill him could be a good reason to kill me."

"Do you want me to put a man with you?"

I shook my head. "I'd only try to lose him, sir."

"Quite so. Just what I'd expect of a good operator." He checked his watched. "Tomorrow night, my men will be rounding up the rest of Turncott's circle at Goodladies Junction. You ought to come along and see the fun."

PART THREE

SHE DESERVES TO BE FAMOUS

TWELVE

Goodladies Road

The Commodore's invitation put me on the edge of a street fight on Goodladies Road. The families who were there say it's still famous. For years to come, I would pretend I was nowhere near. People have heard too many stories about that night. Usually, they are made up – and I know that I was telling fibs before the daylight came. But in 1963, Timberdick Woodcock got the truth out of me. She had taken me swimming in the municipal lido; it was after dark so we needed to break through the fence and we were eventually chased away by Constable Moreton and three council workers. They didn't catch us but Timbers and I spent forty minutes giggling in a ditch while they looked for us. I said it reminded me of the night when I had hidden in the bushes while Irish Dowell undressed. "I've heard about that," Timbers said. "It was the night of the Goodladies Riot." I tried to say that I knew nothing of it but she made me give up the story

The Goodladies street fight of '37 began as three separate scraps which, like little bushfires, burned on their own, then came together in one great conflagration. On any other night each disturbance might have frizzled out, but, coming together, they ignited an explosion of violence across the three streets that make up the red light district of Goodladies Road. It started at eleven o'clock. By a quarter to twelve, no-one could believe what had happened.

My evening began quietly enough. I had enjoyed my day off, sleeping in the Southern Railways library until three in the afternoon. After tea in a signal box, I decided to walk to the road junction and see what I could of the round-up of Turncott's fellow travellers. I wasn't in uniform; Friday night was the start of my rest weekend. I trod along the main road, practising the policeman's dawdle that Martindale had taught me so carefully. As I passed the barracks, I saw two sentries pouring tea for their sergeant in the guard room. A taxi was standing at the rank, the driver had the racing pages folded over the steering wheel. And when I crossed the circus, a flash of torchlight said that I had been recognised by the East Beat officer; he was smoking in the double doors of Dick's coachworks. At the bottom of Goodladies Road, I found a needie called Callan asleep in an alley. I stood and smoked half a Wills, then pressed the left-overs between his fingers. He mumbled and pinched the end and put the fag away for later. I told him that the light was on in Dick's because I knew that the engineer was happy to make him a hot drink at this time of night. It felt like an evening empty of tension. No fathers were drinking. No lovers were arguing. And when a dog barked, a mile off, no other sound obscured its shout across the sky. As I walked slowly round the broad bend and Goodladies Junction came into view, I decided that, if I wasn't home by twelve, I would go back for supper with the lads at the town centre railway station.

Nothing like that happened.

I didn't know it but the first of the bushfires had started to smoulder. Soapy Berkeley had been drinking in the Hoboken Arms. When Irish Dowell delivered a free beer to his out of the way table, he cheekily offered two bob to look up her dress. Others cheered when she slapped him down, insisting that she was worth much more. One joke led to another and Irish eventually declared that for two pints of silver she would take everything off. Most people took it for fun and even when a tankard was passed around, few men put in their shillings with any expectation. Indeed, when Irish saw the collection mount, she declared that all the money would go to the church. "You're wasting your time, boys," she teased. But later in the evening, Berkeley was chuntering, "She said it. Under her breath, I heard it. 'Unless you fill both glasses to the top,' she said."

Outside in the cold, I saw a broken name plate for Bunyards Lane, hanging from the side wall of a terrace. Remembering the Commodore's information about dog fights in a cellar, I walked slowly and quietly down the dark alley. I identified the door to the dungeon at the end of the path but when I was twenty yards from it, two men in open shirts and golden braces stepped forward from nowhere. One carried a blackjack, the other held some lead piping.

"Not for you, sonny. Not down here." The spokesman saw me thinking that I was older than either of them. "Yeah, sonny," he goaded.

"Fine. I was looking for a leak but I can go somewhere else."

"That's right, sonny. Go somewhere else."

But my curiosity wasn't satisfied. I worked out that by climbing the roofs from any adjacent alley, I would be able to reach the cellar by dropping down a gap less than two feet wide between two of the houses. It took me half an hour but I managed to reach the roof I needed without being spotted. I crouched down and saw the two bouncers chewing tobacco. I listened to their grumbling about the cold and the meanness of their bosses. They had heard the stories of Irish Dowell's striptease. One thought she had already done it but the other said not. "Then we ought to see it, Joe. And I don't see why we should pay. Why not go off to the Hoboken and get up to date. Get the when and where, and how's it being done." (This was the first I heard of the nonsense.)

I withdrew from the roof's edge and, like a lizard with two broken legs, I backed myself to the gap over the cellar wall. Carefully, knowing that from now on I'd have no easy escape, I slithered down the brickwork.

I thought I was lucky, to begin with. At the foot of my climb was a small sheet of dirty glass that served as a skylight to the underground room. I squeezed and breathed in until I lay flat in a gully of discarded rubble. I looked inside.

At first, I saw nothing but a forest of sweating men, most were waving their arms. It was so hot that several were stripped to their waists. They were drinking, betting handfuls of money and shouting, but they made no sense to me. I couldn't make out one word; they were all growls and drawls. Three gas jets drew my attention to a little circus ring surrounded by rough and ready fencing, tied together with rope and old dungarees. Outside the ring, benches rose in tiers to the top of the blackened brick walls. The top seats were twelve feet above the ground and so close to the ceiling that men had to lie across them rather than sit up.

I expected to see two pit bulls in the circus but, when the call went up for the next dog, a small white English terrier was let loose on the dirt. A rough looking Scotsman came in, carrying something live in a tied up sack. I didn't know what was happening.

Then this ringmaster, dressed like an old fashioned lock-keeper, spilled dozens of rats from the bag. Hundreds, I thought, but then I told myself off for exaggerating. The terrier set about them with an expertise that staggered me. He caught one in his mouth, broke its neck and tossed it in the air, but he had grasped another before the first hit the ground. For four or five minutes, he went on killing and didn't seem to tire until the job was done.

The man with the sack looked straight at me and bellowed: "Stranger at the window!"

I dropped to the ground, ready for huge hands to reach down and haul me through broken glass, but each man knew that his best resort was to flee the cellar. There was a great rumble as they leapt from the benches and made for the stone steps on the far side of the house. It took them less than four minutes to clear the place and, when I summoned the courage to peer through the window, not a soul was left and cellar was in darkness. I could make out the rows of benches but the kraal had gone and the dead rats had been shovelled away.

Forty men spilled into the streets at the front and back of the building and headed, cursing loudly and ready for a fight, to the junction with Goodladies Road where the Dowell boys were looking for trouble.

The brothers had picked up word that too many men were responding to Berkeley's promise that two glasses of silver would definitely prompt a peepshow from the Dowell's only sister. Soapy had already been thrown out of the pub for breaking wind after warnings, and the brothers were searching the streets for him. Or anyone who had put money in the pot.

The first scuffles broke out when the two mobs met.

At that moment, the Commodore's men dragged three of their prisoners from the Hoboken's dray yard. The subaltern in charge misread the commotion in the open ground of the junction. Believing that the Dowells and the men from the cellar had formed up to ambush his detail, he asked the senior police officer to commence battle. The policeman said he would take advice. But the subaltern didn't wait; he immediately ordered his troop of marines to draw batons and secure his passage down Goodladies Road.

Seconds later, each of the gangs were involved in someone else's fight. It began with yelling and stone throwing and the excited, pointless, kicking of household doors. Street debris was snatched up for weapons as two herds of fifty men faced each other across the junction of five roads. Still, it might have stopped at that if two men hadn't started fighting with knives on the edge of the crowd. The marines pushed forward and the violence broke loose. In no time, a young man was dumped against a wall, blood pouring from his forehead. Another was lying on the ground, unconscious and unnoticed, beneath the feet of the two gangs. There was no command. Men at the back lobbed missiles over the heads of the first rank – not from any sense of formation but because they had no other way of getting at the enemy. Even the terriers at the front thrashed and kicked wildly with no notion of gaining ground or forcing withdrawal; they just wanted to hurt the other side more. Groups of three or four broke away and set about commando tasks of their own, chasing runaways down side streets, dragging obstacles into the middle of the road or braking windows and kicking in gates for more spoil.

The noise of a street brawl is like the belly ache of a stranded beast. Not the yelling and shouting that you hear in the school playground. None of the individual cheers that you get from a football crowd. The roar and rumble is like the vanguard of an army – and all the more frightening for it. I climbed out of my hidey-hole and, from the roofs of Cardrew Street, I saw three householders flag down an omnibus on its way back to the depot. They convinced the driver to abandon it across the entrance to their road so that it formed a makeshift barricade. I remembered Sergeant Martindale's advice that the wrought iron staircase behind Stott's Bakery gave the best view of Goodladies Junction. Then, someone shouted that policemen were mustering at the bottom of 'The Road' where the buses turn around, so, forgetting about Stott's, I dropped into an alley and headed away from the trouble at the junction. I thought that I would join the police team in minutes and be part of a disciplined action, but I had no grasp of the pattern of these little jitties and I was soon lost.

Most of the people in the houses put out their lights, closed their curtains and told their children to keep away from the windows. But more than one old woman wanted to be involved. Several thought I was one of the 'escaping injured'; they rattled their windows open and offered me sanctuary and Horlicks. A grandmother in curlers offered to wash me down; I think that she expected me to go back for another fight once I had been refreshed.

High on the embankment, a goods train stopped between signals, its locomotive panting in the night. I heard a sergeant bring a string of military vehicles to a halt and he started shouting at the engine driver. Surely, he didn't want to commandeer the train?

When, after twenty minutes in dark alleyways, I emerged at the corner of Teggs' tobacco shop, my heart slumped. His shop had been attacked. The mob had moved on, leaving Teggs to sweep up the shattered glass and splintered wood. And the canvas blinds which the mindless thugs had ripped from his windows and burned on the pavement. Once again, I had missed the action. With the resignation of a man who had been through it all before – in other places, in other years – my new friend leant on the broom handle and sighed, "Leave it to me. You better go inside. Your leader, he's a broken man."

The Chief Constable was slumped on the floor in a dark corner of the shop. He had folded his legs so that his head fitted between his knees as he sobbed into a big white handkerchief. "The Commodore's to blame. His crooked sailors could have been arrested in their ships. But no, he wanted it to be public. It's all his fault. It's all, everything, is his fault. It ..." The words withered on their vine.

This was the old colonel who had led his army into the battles of the South African Wars, saluting his soldiers with a sword raised high in the air as he spurred his favourite charger into the teeth of danger. I remembered the Commodore's pencil sketch of those glory days, hanging in the foyer of our headquarters. Now I wanted to put my hand on his shoulder but it seemed impertinent. He was my Chief Constable, after all.

I went out to see Teggs. "I'll help you clear up," I said.

He looked worried. "No, you better go."

"They won't come back," I assured him.

"No, you go."

I remembered Turncott's advice. Stay close to the people and don't turn away from things that are wrong. Was it advice from a traitor? Well, it sounded pretty good to me. I stepped to the kerb, where the streetlights showed me up and people at bedroom windows could hear me speak. "Teggsie, I don't care if these thugs see me helping you. Friends need to stick together at times like this. We should be seen, shoulder to shoulder. Let's make it clear that nothing – no-one – can get in the way of a true friendship."

"You don't understand. My dear Ned, you'll get hurt if you are caught round here."

"I don't care."

Then, with a red face and clenched fists, Mrs Teggs marched out from the shop front. I started to say how sorry I was but she grabbed my collar, drew back an arm and slapped me hard across the face. I fell to my knees.

"God, now stop this," Teggs demanded of us both. He occupied the middle of the pavement and meant to keep us apart by brandishing the business end of the broom. But it was all show.

He wife wanted more. "Animal!" she cried, so fiercely that Teggs stepped aside and she kicked me in the ribs. I rolled into the gutter. Her wedding ring had cut my lip and she had smacked me so hard that now she was nursing her fingers between the shape of her breast and an armpit. "Bringing such filth into my house!" she shouted.

Teggs helped me to my feet. "You better go," he said, his face close up to mine. "My son found the cigarette advertisement and he crayoned in the missing bits. A deep red comma on each big breast. Myself, I'm proud of our boy's imagination. But I couldn't let his mother think that one of her children had done this, so I said it was you."

"And she believed you?"

"It's so believable, Ned. In some ways you are very young."

I stepped towards her. "Mrs Teggs ..."

"Don't speak to me!" She had a tiger in her, made more scary by the streetlight reflected in her eyes and the icy perspiration on her face. She bared her teeth. "Animal! I don't want to hear that you're sorry. You are worse than any of the ruffians who broke our shop to pieces. What you did – bringing such vulgar dirt into our home for our children to see – it's so much worse. You are a beast! Go back to your jungle, Mr Machray." And she waved a hand towards Goodladies Junction.

"Mrs Teggs ..."

Her husband tugged at my sleeve. "You'd better go, Ned. Time, in these things, is a good healer but right now I think you make matters worse."

Thank heavens the Chief was so wrapped up in his own misery that he didn't intervene. Surely, he had heard the commotion. Who could have missed it? But if he made any sense of it, he decided that it was all too much of a nuisance. When I looked through the open door, he was still crying and he didn't see me.

"You shouldn't have told her, Teggsie."

"What could I do?" He put an arm around my shoulder and began to walk me away.

"I need to find the other policemen," I said. "They are forming up where the buses turn."

"No, no. Go home, my friend."

"But the other policemen?"

"Let's say they've disbanded thirty minutes ago. Did they go back to their stations?" He shrugged. "I don't know."

I heard a roar and a rumble, half a mile up the road. "Then I'll go back to Goodladies Junction," I said.

He took his arm away and stood in the middle of the road as I walked on. "Ned, keep away from it all. You are not a man for nights like this. My friend, my good friend, listen to me, yes?"

My father always said that the Great War was different from other wars because the soldier had no room to run. My grandfather, who had served in the Zulu campaigns, had described the distant thunder of battle in adjacent valleys and how a warrior's shriek could soar across heavenly blue horizons like an arrow from a pagan god. Some other poor fellows were fighting. But in Flanders, my father said, the cannon fire was never anyone else's. It always belonged to you in your black hell. Always, all the ground shook and all the sky cracked and a soldier couldn't run from the horror. That's what gave men the shimmies, he said.

That night, as I walked up Goodladies Road for the second time, I remembered my grandfather's descriptions. There was shouting, stone throwing and crashing but, although it was near, it didn't seem likely to involve me. I had been in the neighbourhood throughout the street fight but I had done nothing to boast about. An angry housewife had thrown me into the gutter and I had disturbed a dog fight, sending scores of angry men into the street and looking for trouble. When I hadn't been looking down from rooftops, I had been scurrying down back alleys. I had spent most of my time looking for a police squad so that I could join in. Now, Teggs wanted me to pretend that they had given up the fight and gone home.

At one moment, I could hear fighting half a mile up the road, but behind the houses on the left side. But, in the next moment, the turmoil seemed at a much closer latitude but further east. It was as if I was being drawn into a valley with tribes on either side and, if I kept my head down, they wouldn't touch me.

That confidence took a knock when I reached the junction with Yarns Lane (a cobbled stretch with no light and no way out at the bottom). A woman in grey clothes was sitting cross-legged in the gutter, her thighs bare up to her knickers. I could see that she had badly twisted her ankle and her dress had been ripped from her shoulders. She had finished crying, although her face was wet with tears. She was trying to use her knees to support her elbows as she tried to tend to her scalp, but her knees kept breaking down so her arms gave way. She wanted her fingers to stem the bleeding from the side of her head. The red had soaked her yellow hair and her hands were covered in it.

As I knelt to help her, she saw the marks on my face and winced in sympathy. "Six buggers," I fibbed "They had me up against the arches. I gave as good at I got."

"My bloke didn't stand a chance either. Silly sod went in head first and got it cracked open." She craned forward, her eyes narrowed. I guessed that she had lost her spectacles. "I don't know you, do I?" she asked.

"I'm the new copper around here."

"Shit!" She edged up against the wall. "You're the one with VD!"

"No, no. I'm clear now. Absolutely."

But she didn't want to risk it. She shook her head.

"How far have you come?" I asked.

Before she could answer, a beer bottle smashed on the brick wall above us. A great shout went up as a posse of thugs with flails and clubs surged from the opposite pavement. I braced her shoulders and, regardless of her protests in pain, I dragged her further into the dark of the alley. But the gang wanted to keep to the main road; they left us alone, except for three who promised to finish us.

As their animal taunts grew more urgent, I sat the girl against the wall and a dug a handkerchief from my pocket. For a moment when our faces were close together, I recognised the look in her cold eyes. She knew what was going to happen and she knew that she could do nothing about it.

At first, they kept three or four paces off, enjoying our discomfort.

"Get going," they said to me. "We're not looking for you."

I stood my ground. Behind me, the girl was crying on the pavement and a husband and wife were hiding behind their scullery curtain.

"You'll get hurt and we've nothing against you."

They were all about twenty years old and had forty stones between them. Most of that was muscle. The yellow haired one had a bicycle chain wrapped around his knuckles; the others two had old police truncheons. I stepped forward, putting myself between them and the girl. When they warned me for the third time, I reached behind for a clutch of the girl's dress sleeve and pulled her up. She was weak on her feet; I knew that we couldn't run. She wouldn't have made fifty yards.

'Sandy' pushed his mates aside, elbowed me out of the way and lunged forward. He got his hands to the girl's neck and dug both thumbs into her throat. I yelled at him and kicked. He took it in the kidneys, arched backwards and threw a wild punch at me as he fell.

The second in command thought about moving in. I stopped that with a knuckled fist to his nose. I threw it with all my strength, knowing that I had only one go. The third kid was already going for the girl. I stuck out a foot and sent him sprawling. But Sandy was on his feet again. He wrapped me in his arms and turned me to face his accomplices. I pushed back and threw both legs in the air but it was a waste. My strength had gone and my foot smashed against a stone drain cover.

The girl was screeching like a penned parrot. We were done for. I had nothing left, my ankle was injured and the three against us were fighting fit. I managed to smack an elbow against the kitchen window, hoping that the couple would come out. They stayed silent.

Then the man who had me in the bear-hug started to choke. I broke free as he went down against the wall. He was vomiting.

"Look after him!" I shouted. "He's bloody hurt, can't you see!"

His friend hesitated before accepting my truce, then he knelt at his friend's side. The other one flung himself at the girl, in one last go. I struck his nose again, knowing that it had connected well when I felt the cave-in of gristle and splintered bone. Two hands covered his face as blood dribbled between his fingers. All he could make was a gurgling nose as he crawled around on his elbows and knees.

I dragged the girl to the porch and hammered on the door, shouting 'Police' and 'Open up' like they were the only lines I knew. I heard the rattle of chains and latches, the door opened just a couple of inches but I kicked it free and tossed the sobbing girl inside. "Look after her!" I didn't have to wait for the door to slam shut.

* * *

I found a dead end in Rossington Street with two railway cottages set back from the pavement, overshadowed by the viaduct and the back of Towney's warehouse. I put myself down on a doorstep and tried to keep my poorly foot off the ground. The ankle was already swelling and I was sure that I'd broken it. I thought that I could hear some dance music, far off, but I could hear no people on the streets. The usual din came from the freight yard and there was a hideous winding noise from a heavy crane. Then I heard a curious wail floating up from the earth. It took me some minutes to puzzle it out. The Tupner family was singing prayers in the next door cottage.

Shaking Jacobs came shambling up from a footpath. "I've got us a lift, Mr Mac. Sid's coal cart is waiting on the other side of the viaduct. We've got to cross the footbridge, that's all."

"I'll never be able to do that," I complained.

"Then I'll find you a stick," he said and went off again.

Forty minutes had passed before Jacobs and Mike the mechanic lifted me onto the back of the empty coal wagon. My foot had been bandaged with dirty rags from the gutter and a make-do crutch was wedged under one armpit.

"Don't let Elsie see you in this state," said Mike. "I've seen her ring a peacock's neck for having a game leg." The three of us were sitting with our backs to the timber bulkhead. Sid's mare stood contentedly between the shafts.

"No, you didn't," Jacobs protested. "You're saying what people have told you but you didn't see it yourself. She didn't kill the peacock. She told Berkeley what had to be done. And she said it because it was the kindest thing."

"Aye, she's dead kind, that one," said a rough voice. I turned around and saw the coalman approaching from the shadows. "She's still going to do it, she says, but it's got to be out of the way. She says, the veranda in the bat and ball park."

Jacobs explained that he was talking about Irish Dowell, not Elsie. Sidney flicked the reins and the chestnut started to walk slowly though the night. The gangs had gone but neighbours were wary of coming out onto the pavements, so the roads were empty. Our horse took the middle of the road, paid no attention to crossroads or rights of way and clip-clopped at her own unhurried pace.

"A pleasant evening," someone observed.

"And easy company too."

"Yes," I agreed, taking in the air. "Very pleasant."

Mike turned his attention to a old flagon, hidden under some straw, and with our help – the thing was very heavy – he poured four beakers of beer. "What you'd give for one of Elsie's hot muffins now, eh, PC Machray?"

My tongue went around my mouth, checking for that tacky taste of the cold muffins she had fed me on the night of the murder. "The ale will do fine," I said.

After all the turmoil, our cart ride through the city after midnight was a curious, rustic interlude. I started to hum Mother Dowell's tune about tough men in the Wild West. A trumpeter called Nat Gonella had recently recorded it so it was easily recognised. Michael started to whistle along and Shaking knew some of the words. Sid joined in when he could. It was all a very light effort and we managed to keep time with the horse's hoofs. As we passed under a railway bridge, Davy Tupner, up top, threw down some apples and shouted that we should sing up. I think that spoilt it a little.

"Do you want to know what she did to the peacock when it was dead?" asked Mike. "Well, she roasted it."

"Dead tasty, roasted peacock," Sid said over his shoulder.

Mike agreed. "But I say it's not a thing a lady would want to do. Roasting such a beautiful bird. Peacocks look like royalty with all those feathers. No, as far as I'm concerned, roasting a peacock is the mark of a cruel woman."

"Mr Wycherley was always kind to animals," said Shaking. "Even on the night he died, he brought the cat into the Palfreyman for her milk."

"No, he didn't." Mike objected.

"That's what I said. No, he didn't."

"You're making no sense," I said. "Anyway, you weren't there, Shaking."

"Well then, I wouldn't know, would I?" he conceded and sniffed the hops in his beer. "But Elsie said Mrs Ritchers told him to put it on the floor before he took his beer. That's what Rosie told her, anyway."

I asked what the street fight had been about.

"What do you think? Communists and fascists? A crooked bookie."

Jacobs cut in. "No, it was over a woman."

"Young Irish Dowell. She promised the men in the Hoboken Arms a peek-a-boo show, if we filled a pint mug with money. We thought she was joking but when her brothers heard about it, they threatened to break the arms of any man who put a coin in the tankard. When the word got out, the three big families took sides."

Sid said, "Well, I've heard that the owner of the Cockatoo started it. He wanted to take over the sporting dogs and the boys in Bunyard Lane would have none of it." He called over his shoulder, "Do you want dropping at Elsie's?"

"No, the cathedral, I think. I think I might sit in the grounds for a while."

"You're not welcome at Elsie's, then?" Mike asked. "What have you been up to?"

"No, no. I just fancy a sit."

"Aw, lad," drawled the driver, "Why not come along with us? The cricket field is hardly three miles from here."

So far, the ride had been so comfortable and the company so friendly that I accepted their invitation with no thought of the consequences.

THIRTEEN

Irish Dowell

Sidney snapped, "Stop fidgeting, Jacobs!" and took a third look through his binoculars. We were lying four abreast in long grass. I was the only one without a pair of glasses.

"I don't know why we're hiding," Shaking sniffed. "She knows we're here, that's what we paid for."

"Do you want her brothers to see us?" Michael explained.

"And I don't want the others to spot us." Sidney tried to make out what was happening in the bushes on the far side of the cricket pitch. "Keep quiet, Shaky. You've got a voice like a startled lark. I'll never take you duck shooting."

"I'd never want to go duck shooting," Jacobs sulked. "Not with you, anyhow."

"Mike, can you see anything?"

The mechanic replied without taking the field glasses from his face. "Can't we get any closer?"

Sidney agreed. "We're not in the best position."

"Young Berkeley's over there with the dustbins," said Jacobs. "When Irish comes onto the veranda, he'll get some great views from the back. He'll be close enough to blow kisses, I think."

Sydney told him to be quiet.

A young woman with red hair and an evening dress walked out of the pavilion and hung an oil lamp from a beam across the veranda. She went away and came back with another. She did it half a dozen times until the wooden decking was lit like a school play.

Jacobs said, "I don't like what Berkeley's up to. He's bobbing up and down."

Sid told him to be quiet.

"Really, Mr Ned. I think you ought to get over there."

I detached myself from the pals and dragged my bruised ankle over the bushes and ditches that marked the boundary of the field. By the time I reached the pavilion, I had lost sight of Berkeley and tinny jazz music was spilling over from a wind-up gramophone perched on the edge of the veranda. I was twenty yards from her when Irish reached up high to adjust the oil lamps. Suddenly, she squealed, "Ow!" and brought both hands down to hold her dress close to her legs. "Who's flicking stones?" she snapped. I knew that I would be the likely suspect so I dropped to the muddy grass and crawled the rest of the way.

I slithered between the stilts, beneath the pavilion's floor. I could hear the girl doing her phoney ballet on the veranda; the place shook every time she jumped, then she would wait a few moments before moving again. She wanted to be sure that the wooden shack wasn't going to fall down. (I was just as worried that the oil lamps would drop to the floor and set us all alight.) I had aggravated my ankle and couldn't trust it with any weight so my progress was like a lazy crocodile who'd lost his sense of direction. Nettles and thistles and knobs of flint scratched my arms and legs. At one stage, I was so bound up that I had to stop and break the stalks off me. I don't know how many times my skull knocked against the timber floorboards above me, but I was surely making enough row to wake the dead. The soggy mud had soaked through to my knees and elbows and I was becoming uncomfortably aware that my face was caked with dirt. I tasted clay soil in my mouth. 'You'll look like an Indian Scout,' I told myself. But, no, I'd be no more than a fat boy who had been playing too long on the rubbish dump. (I could imagine what bossy Elsie would have to say about that.) I knew that Soapy Berkeley was scampering around the outside of the pavilion, giggling and squawking; he was up to no good. I had an awful feeling that I had got caught up with so many odd characters that the night was bound to end in humiliation. "I'll settle for that," I caught myself whispering. "Humiliation will do." I feared something worse.

At last, I came up from the underground and felt the cold night air on my face. I didn't know where I was, exactly, so I rubbed my eyes – and Irish Dowell's bottom in cheap cotton knickers passed in front of my nose.

I had emerged onto a patch of long grass where the veranda protruded from the keep of the pavilion. When I stood up, the veranda was waist high, making the lady's bottom just right for the middle of my face. She still had her clothes on but she was holding up her dress to show off her legs and underwear.

Even now, I remember her bottom as one of the finest I have found. It filled her grey pants like a near perfect pudding. A little doughie. A trifle fleshy. But all that was laid over a foundation of good and strong muscle. It looked like gluteus maximus sounds. It was a bottom to paint, to sculpt or thumb into shape in soft clay. It was almost impossible not to touch.

"Oi! What are you doing there? A greasy Billy Bunter, if ever I saw one!"

The lanterns gave a touch of gold to her clean face and pinned up hair.

"Miss Dowell, I need to talk to you."

"No! Go back to the others. That's where you ought to be, with the others. Did you pay extra?"

"Your mother said I should ask you."

"Ask me what? No, she didn't."

"About Rosie Ditchen in the alley."

"Oh God! Oh God, you're the copper with the pox. Get away from me. Ow!" She slapped her hands to her bottom as if she had been bitten by something in the night. "Was that you?"

"And why did you visit Hubert Wycherley on the night he died?"

"Did I?"

"Annie Ankers saw you at the window and I found your cocktail glass."

"He wanted to ask me about something Polly had told him, that's all. It's nothing to do with you."

"About the murder in her loft?"

"Look, it wasn't in her loft. God, I mean, it wasn't anywhere. Look, it was poor Polly's cock up. She'd lured Hubert to her loft and told him that silly murder story. She said that I knew something about it, so Hubert wanted to ask me. Ouch!" She slapped her bottom hard. "Are you flicking things at my arse?"

"Did you see it? Did you see the murder?"

125

"You are you doing it, aren't you? Firing stones at me."

"Of course, I'm not. You can see me. I'm just standing here, watching you."

"Well, somebody's being bloody funny."

"Did you see the murder?" I persisted.

"No! Look, there was no murder. How many times do you need telling?"

"But Polly told Hubert you knew?"

"My dear mother had already told Polly that I knew a secret about Rosie. Polly thought that she meant, you know, that Rosie had done it. Except there was no murder in the first place and what I saw had nothing to do with it, even if there was."

"You mother said that you found Rosie Ditchen robbing a sailor."

"That's my secret. Nothing to do with the stupid murder. Christ! That was you again." Now she was leaning to one side, nursing a nick to her thigh.

"Please, don't stop dancing. Carry on. It was ... lovely."

She skipped to the other end of the platform, crossed her hands in front of her dress, took hold of the hem and, in one movement, lifted the garment over her head and away from her. A distant chorus of cheers wafted across the darkened cricket green; speckles of torchlight were all that I could see of Sidney and the boys.

She came back to me, leaned forward a little, and folded her hands behind to unbutton her brassiere.

"It was two in the morning in the back alley between the Hoboken and the railway." Her hands fell away and two warlike breasts came to attention. Less than ten inches from my face. "Rosie Ditchen and Elsie were bending over the trawler captain. Drunk and out for the count, he was. He didn't know what was happening."

"They were taking his money?"

"They were sharing it out when I saw them. Elsie was grumbling because Rosie took most of it. I think that's what was going on." She turned her back to me and slowly took her last piece of clothing down to her ankles.

Irish Dowell undressed in '37 was beyond storytelling. "You're lovely," I said and her bottom wiggled, just a little. It lasted for no more than a firefly's heartbeat but, in that moment, I thought I had grown up at last. Why had I been looking at older women when young ladies like this were out and about? Elsie with her muffins was a grandma compared to Miss Dowell.

"Ouch!" She shot up straight. "Ow!" And she clasped both hands to her bottom.

Then the needle scratched over the record grooves, leaving the click-click-clicking as the turntable wound down. We both turned to see what had disturbed the music and inane giggle came up from the veranda fence. Soapy Berkeley's weasel face appeared. "It wasn't me," he whined. (I conjured up a picture of a schoolboy who produced those words whenever something went awry.)

"Soapy! You vicious bugger. It bloody hurts!" she shouted.

He waggled his child's pea-shooter at her. "I'll wait until you're facing me and not ready," he teased. "Then I'll do it some more. I bet I'll get your doi-dois, first go!"

She ran across the timber boards.

"For Gawd's Sake, arrest me, Ned. For my own good. Arrest me before she kills me."

* * *

He promised to come quietly if we avoided Central Police Station. "Someone ought to write an opera about them," he said as we walked along the pavement to the little nick at the bottom of Baltry Road.

"Yes," I said, thinking about it.

"Someone German ought to write an opera about them."

"Yes."

Twenty yards ahead, two large constables marched out of the police station, crossed the road and went the other way without turning their heads.

Soapy breathed, "Germanic breasts."

"Keep quiet, Soapy. Don't go on about it."

"How do girls do that?" he asked. "Take off their dresses in one go without getting snagged. Do mothers teach them when they're young? Or is it something they're born with? Part of their natural allure, do you think?" He considered the matter and decided: "They practise in front of mirrors. On their own, in front of mirrors."

"Stop thinking about it, Soapy."

"For years. They do it for years. It's wicked, the way they practise and practise just to catch us. Capture our will, that's what they do." Then, as we walked up the steps to the station, he said, "You're nervous, lad. You've not done this before, have you?"

"Why have you brought this man to my police station?" demanded the sergeant at the charging lectern. Ernest Berkeley had been right; he was my first arrest so I thought that the formal tone was the company way of doing things. But then I noticed the time – it was a quarter to two in the morning and the skipper didn't want to be bothered with a prisoner when he was ready to go off duty.

"He was shooting pellets at Irish Dowell's bottom," I said

"Pellets?"

"From a pea-shooter, Sergeant."

"At her bottom?"

"Her bare bottom, Sergeant."

"And you were close enough to see?"

"I was very close, Sergeant. There's no doubt."

"And that's what you're going to tell the magistrate, is it? You were close to Irish Dowell's bottom ..."

" Bare bottom, Corp," Berkeley emphasised.

" ... when Berkeley shot his pea at it." He slapped the charge ledger shut. "You better do him for drunk and incapable," he said, pushing a printed form into my hand. "Empty your pockets, Berkeley."

While my prisoner placed his possessions on the lectern – coins, penknife, a length of string, three loose matches and half a cigarette – I read the evidence which I was required to sign. I needed to write the time, date and place of the arrest; otherwise evidence for all drunks was the same and prepared on one neatly typed page. Drunks were unable to stand, smelled of wine and spoke in a slurred manner. But none of these characteristics applied to my Mr Berkeley.

The sergeant noticed my hesitation. "You'll take a drunk charge, won't you Berkeley?"

"Anything to oblige, Corporal. Do you want me to sign for my prop?"

"Too drunk to sign," the sergeant articulated as he wrote the appropriate certificate in the day book. "Cell Number Three. Keep quiet and we won't lock you in."

* * *

On my way from the cells, I noticed an old auxiliary working on files beneath a desk lamp. I stepped into the dingy office, intending to ask about dog fights in the city, when a letter on the table caught my eye.

"I'm weeding," said the pensioner without looking up. "Sorting out those old papers that can be thrown away. That's a letter from a headmaster who thought one of his old boys was going to cause trouble. Years ago." He lifted a corner of the page to check. "Four years ago."

I was reading the neat italic handwriting. The name of the former pupil was Louis Bloire – the name in Davy Tupner's jacket.

"He probably was," I said. "He had a knife pocket sewn into his coat."

"Four years ago. There was a story that he had been murdered in Blackamore Lane but it was all bunkum. Arnie Gutterman did a thorough investigation and there was nothing in it. Drop the letter on the pile for burning."

"After only four years?"

"It's dangerous to leave that sort of letter on file. You never know who might come looking for it. Enquiries. Complaints. Letters from Parliament. You never know."

"Can I hold on to it?"

"No, you can't. Leave it there for burning."

FOURTEEN

Annie's Answer

The cathedral cat was hurrying home; home, that is, to the discarded coal shovel wedged against a sunken door at the side of the church through which she could squeeze and drop to a forgotten cellar. Her mind was so caught up with the promise of the stale odours and warmth of the place that she hardly slowed down when she ducked into the great bush at the cathedral gates and emerged, just seconds later, with a dead mouse in her mouth. (Earlier in the evening, she had been disappointed by the vermin's weight and had left it there, hoping for something better. Now, she would take it home and chew on it. For amusement, really. She hadn't any hunger for such skin and bones.) The rooks, the mongrel and the city hares kept an eye on her. None of the creatures liked her, this cat who had to have her own way and wouldn't be told. Her sins would find her out, one day.

The cat stopped where two church paths crossed and put her head to one side. The tower was eerie with the silence of rooks keeping a special watch and, instead of sleeping in the stone porch, the mongrel was resting uneasily on the steps to the chlorifier. They had seen my quiet figure come slowly – round shouldered and shuffling – to the stone porch. Now, the cat had to decide what to do about my trespass. She disappeared into the shadows on the long grass but reappeared, close to the church entrance.

She stared at me.

Ah, you don't know what to do, I thought. Frighten or befriend me? Fool me? Or make the most of my presence?

As if to teach me a lesson, the uncomfortable taste of Elsie's warmed up muffins came back to my mouth. The murder was five days old now, like the muffins, but I couldn't get rid of the taste of the doughie mix. Nonsense. Absolute nonsense. But what was it that kept me thinking about Monday night's muffins?

From Cathedral Close, Annie Ankers' almshouse looked dead. But when I went around the back, the curtains were open and I saw Annie drinking in the glow of a standard lamp. She'd got her nightdress on, slippers but no dressing gown and she'd spent forty minutes doing her hair. Just in case somebody dropped by, I supposed. She said, "My husband's not in," and waved at me. I managed to get a window open from the outside. "You don't have to climb in," she said. "You could walk through the door like anyone else."

"Is that what anyone does, Annie? I don't think that would be very proper."

"Come in, Constable. I said my husband's not here. Come in and you can have whiskey on my hearthrug."

I stayed at the window, but I got my pipe from my pocket and filled it with Teggs Special Mixture, just to be sociable. "That cat's still prowling round the churchyard," I said. I leant on the window ledge so that my elbow and nose were in the house and the rest of me was standing out in the cold.

"Please don't light your pipe, Constable. The smoke will linger and Josh'll think that I've had a man in the house. Though why shouldn't I?"

"That's – no, I couldn't. I mean, it would be bad manners to sneak into a man's house without him knowing."

"And what about making love to his wife? How rude is that?"

"Please, don't talk like this."

Then she leaned forward to say, "Don't worry. Mother Dowell says there's nothing wrong with you. She only cleaned you up because she wants you to be beholden to her. You see, do you?"

"You mean, I haven't got VD."

"Never had, so she says. Do you know what I think?"

I shook my head. "No," and I wanted it to stay that way.

"I think the crafty old mare just wanted to take a good look at you."

I didn't know what to make of that. "It's good news," I said. "That I haven't got it, I mean."

"I say, you couldn't go back to Elsie's for your uniform, could you?"

"Difficult. I'm not really staying at Elsie's. She thinks I keep looking up her skirt."

I wasn't sure that she'd heard me.

"Oh, what a dream for a young girl," she said wistfully. "Sitting alone, drinking, with nothing over her nightie, when a policeman in his uniform appears at the window. Ooh, it's just the sort of thing you read in naughty novels. Have you read the ones by Paul Renin? All That Glitters is my favourite. A girl with no clothes is bathing on the cover and a gentleman comes down to the lake to spy on her. What happens next, do you think?" She rose from the chair, disappeared into the kitchen and, moments later, emerged on the back door step. She stood so that the breeze pushed her nightdress against the contours of her little underfed body. Her skin was white and dry and her flesh looked easy to bruise.

"Have you ever thought how difficult it is to see your own bottom?"

"Annie, please. I ought to make a joke about that but, please, go back indoors." By now, I had got my pipe going and was looking for somewhere to sit in the back yard. Being an almshouse, the square of concrete had tight little green plants in it.

"You want us to go back to talking through the open window? Well, I managed to get two mirrors on my landing and I had a look." She took a drink. "My cheeks sit unevenly against each other, like two craggy rocks pressed up, on higher than the other, in a mountain range. My legs don't seem to grow out of my bottom at all. Instead, they're puny cocktail sticks stuck in knobs of crumbly old cheese. From the back, I looked very breakable, very breakable indeed."

I smiled, shaking my head.

"Ah, I see. You're thinking of Irish Dowell's nice bottom and mine sounds nothing like hers. 'This old crow ought to go back indoors.' Is that right?"

"Good Lord, you really do have a gift of second sight, don't you?"

"Not really," she admitted with a sigh of resignation. "Josh was on the cricket field, watching her just like you were. I heard him talking to another scoundrel before they went off to rustle for hares."

She went back into the house, shutting the scullery door and making a great deal of noise until she appeared in the sitting-room again. She opened the window wide, reminded me not to poke my head in while I smoked, and installed herself beneath the standard lamp with a fresh glass of whiskey. "I didn't think you'd peep at poor Irish, Ned Machray. Really, I'm disappointed." (But we both knew that she was tickled rather than disappointed.) "Now I think that Elsie might be right about Ned Machray; he looks up ladies' skirts."

"Well, she's not," I objected. "In fact, Elsie isn't right about a lot of things."

"What does she say about Irish?"

"That she could murder someone because she'd expect to get away with it. She says the same about the mother."

"Oh yes. Oh, interesting. And what does she say about me?"

"If you murdered someone, you would need to confess. Rosie would do it to put things right and Elsie would do it because she's a bully."

"Well, yes. She is a bully. Tell me, have you answered the most important question yet? Who shouted murder?"

I drew on my pipe, then tapped the stem against my front teeth.

"Shaking Jacobs," she said.

"But he says he wasn't there."

"Well, Mrs Ritchers told Wycherley that two gentlemen were waiting for him, and she would know. I think it's important to remember what people said at the time, don't you?"

She allowed me a few moments with my thoughts.

"The question is," she prompted. "Why would he deny it when so many people knew he was there?"

I knocked out my pipe. "Why on earth do people call you silly Annie?" I smiled.

"Oh, I think I keep things simple, don't you?"

She had known. All along she had known. We looked at each other and she smiled as the pictured cleared for me.

"My God," I said very quietly.

Oh yes, she was nodding.

"But that means Elsie's in danger. I must get to her!"

* * *

It had passed everyone's bedtime but the road to the crossroads still wasn't empty. Two lovers were squeezing each other in someone else's doorway. She was rubbing the top of his thigh with her knees which poked out from under her skirt. The man didn't see me, the first time, but she did. She was watching everything. Ten yards further on, a drunk had collapsed outside the window of a terraced house. He was asleep but couldn't get comfortable; he tried to roll over but could only manage a snort – like an overweight sea lion.

I needed to cross the road but, when I got half way, the floosie pulled herself back from her bloke and the drunk kicked out, sending a broken bottle into the gutter. It shouldn't have put me off, but it did. I went back to my side of the road. And I didn't like the way the clouds kept changing the colours on the ground. What could we count on, if even that was wrong?

Then I heard the police whistle.

I ran, stopped dead, marched forward a couple of steps, then dithered again. The whistle was so shrill that it carried across half a dozen streets but it was difficult to work out its direction.

The lovers stood apart on the pavement. "The quays!" shouted the youth.

"He says it's coming from the quays," the tart repeated. "You've got to get down to the quays."

I started to run down the middle of the road. The young man decided that he ought to help. He slipped away from the girl and started to jog after me. At that moment, the drunk stirred, got onto all fours and reversed into the other man's path. They collided and rolled along the ground.

The tart had seen enough. She got off the streets, took off her high heels and ran down a side alley. Her footsteps were silent but I heard her yelp when the whistle screeched across the sky again, though it was nowhere near her.

As the crossroads came closer, I saw something had been dumped against the graveyard wall. It looked like a bundle of blankets and old clothes.

Annie had seen it too. "I've got her!" She came running from her house, barefoot and holding her nightdress up to her thighs. "Go on, Ned! Get after the Captain! I'll look after our Elsie."

I raced across the graveyard and into the crooked lanes that led down to the quay. The lanes were so narrow that I bounced off the edges of houses and tripped over kerbs. My ankle began to play up again, so I was hobbling – and close to tears – by the time I reached the harbour.

Already, the Tra'lee was leaving port, a turmoil of water churning from its stern. I ran to the edge and shouted at her to come back. The skipper in the wheelhouse waved a goodbye.

Bugger.

"There's no point to petulance, PC Machray," said a weakened voice. Sergeant Martindale had collapsed against a pile of old railway sleepers. His leg stuck out at a hideous angle; I knew that it was broken. "She was calling for you, Ned. She's against the church wall and badly beaten up, I'm afraid."

I knelt beside him. "I'll stay with you, Serge, until somebody comes."

"Don't be stupid. There's a pub on the dockside. Go and summon two ambulances. One for Elsie, one for me. Then get yourself back to the cathedral and see if you can help her. I'll be all right until the medics get here."

"What about the captain of that trawler?"

"Well, I don't think we can do anything about him now, do you?"

I didn't want to give in so easily. "I'll see that he's brought to justice, one day."

The sergeant laughed. "I'm sure you will."

I dodged my way around the railway wagons, piles of rope and old clothing. Then, when I was between things and couldn't see properly, the new bomber made a low pass over the harbour. I turned to look up and my ankle gave way. "Bloody thing," I cursed as I landed on my backside. "It's not necessary, this time of night."

I got to the fisherman's inn on the quayside and cried, "Open up!" as I hammered on the door. At first, I thought no-one was at home. But I was sure that the landlady with the pig's throat lived on the premises. I tried again, "Open up in the name of the law!"

An upstairs window clattered open and a man poked his bald head out. "I can't hear you!"

"Rubbish!" I yelled at him. "You can, or you wouldn't have opened the window." What took you so long, I wanted to ask.

He wasted more time fitting rimless spectacles on his nose. "All right. I could hear you shouting, but I can't hear what you're going to say next."

I stamped my foot at him. "I haven't said anything yet!"

"Of course you haven't!" he shouted back. "That's what 'next' means!" He put his head back in but returned after a few seconds, placing a home made contraption of wires and batteries on the window ledge. He put one end of a wire in his ear. "Now what's this? The name of the law?" he queried. "You've been watching too many Dick Turpin films, boyo!"

I tried a different approach. "Please, sir. I need to telephone for an ambulance. I mean, two ambulances. My sergeant has broken his leg and there's an injured woman in the graveyard."

"Try your joke on some other idiot, son. You can't be clever with Desmond Pickle because he won't fall for it. There's scores of injured people in graveyards. Very injured, I'd say."

"Please, make the call."

"I'll call for the lady, but not for any sergeant. If he gets drunk, then it's his look out."

"Please, he's not drunk. Please, can I come in and make the call?"

"Certainly not. My wife's in bed." He closed the window and turned off the lights.

I returned to the railway sleepers and found Soapy Berkeley tending to Sergeant Martindale.

"He's called for the medics," Martindale explained as he sipped from a tankard of cold beer.

Berkeley had bandaged the leg with old rags he had found on the quay. "Everything's fine. Annie has taken Elsie into her place and I'll stay with the corporal until the ambulance gets here."

I said, almost timidly. "You're supposed to be in the cells."

"Then I'd say it's a good job I'm not. I don't think we need you anymore, PC Mach. Is there something you can be getting on with?"

Five minutes later, with both hands in the pockets of my civvie trousers, I walked slowly across the cobbled close and through the wrought iron gates of the cathedral yard. I sat on the familiar stone bench and waited for the clock to chime the three-quarter hour. I didn't want to think about much at all.

Now it was clear to me who killed the Dean's Clerk. I only wished that I had been able to work it out before Elsie had been attacked.

I looked for the cat and the dog but saw no signs of life. Even the crows had withdrawn into the brickwork. Then, as blatantly as ever, the moggy pranced up the gravel path with fresh prey in her mouth. The poor church mouse was still alive but too terrified to move. He knew that a struggle would likely snap his neck between her two jaws. His only prayer was to keep alert and dart free if ever the cat relaxed her grip. But each night had made the cat a better hunter and who was to say that she would make a mistake this time? Life was a bloody wretched business. When it got to five-to and still the church hadn't chimed, I remembered what the landlady on the quay had said. No-one had heard the cathedral clock since the death of the Dean's Clerk.

I was sitting on the bench with my collar unbuttoned and my belt loosened as the ambulance men arrived from the Royal Marine depot. Two orderlies got out and went into the Ankers' place. A police Austin stopped at the crossroads and two sergeants got out. Then two constables appeared on foot. One stood sentry at the junction while the other guarded the Ankers' front door.

It was half past before anyone sat down beside me. The Commodore was spruced up and ready for action. Well buttered, my mother would have called him. "You reported that a Naval Captain is involved?"

I kept my head down as I shook it. "No, a trawler skipper."

"The Tra'Lee?"

"She'll be out of your grasp by now."

"Well, maybe but maybe not. Can you tell me what happened?"

When I hesitated, he said gently, "Your Chief's in no condition to lead a serious investigation and every inspector and sergeant wants to curse the day you joined their force. Really, there is no-one else to tell. You tell me what's happened and I'll find a way of saying it's my business." He added, "You're a good man, Constable Machray."

"The trawler captain taught Elsie a lesson; he'd found out that she robbed him."

"He needs to hang," said the Commodore.

I said, "No. But Elsie does, I'm afraid."

FIFTEEN

A Coppersworth

"Elsie? As well as Rosie Ditchen?"

"No, instead of her. Let Rosie go, Commodore. She's served you well."

"Rosie's not under arrest," he assured me. "But she's been in hospital since Turncott attacked her. I've asked them to keep her there."

The orderlies were carrying Elsie out on a tubular framed chair. They parked her on the pavement while they opened the heavy duty doors of the military ambulance. The Commodore told me that I needed to talk to her before they took her to hospital so I followed him to the ambulance.

They had put a cup of tea in her hands and covered her blouse with a tea towel so that no-one would see the blood. Her lips were swollen and her nose had been gashed. "It's much better now," she said, awkwardly, as I knelt beside the chair. "I needed a hot drink, that's all." But her eyes could only stay with me for a few moments before she lost control of them and they fell away to one side, then to the other. Her hands were cold and shivering and she flinched when I touched one wrist. "It's my shoulder mainly," she said. "I don't think that's going to get better at all. Please be sorry for me."

Then I looked at Elsie's pale face and said simply, "It was the taste of the cold muffins. I couldn't get rid of it. Every time I tried to work things out, that taste would come back to my mouth and wouldn't go away. You see, usually they were piping hot – fresh from the oven – but you served them cold on the night Wycherley died. Of course, you did. If you put the muffins in the oven before you left, they'd be burnt by the time you got back. But if you cooked them on your return,

139

you'd have to explain to me where you'd been. So, you had them baked before. That's why they were cold when I tasted them. Cold muffins, Elsie?" I shook my head. "They just weren't your way."

"You think I killed Bert Wycherley?"

The Commodore whispered. "That doesn't prove anything, Ned. It shows that Elsie could have been away from her house. It doesn't place her at the Palfreyman and it doesn't mean that she killed Wycherley."

"Elsie, you tried to throw suspicion on Shaking Jacobs, didn't you?" I said.

"Oh, did I?" She looked at the Commodore and then the orderlies. "Do I have to listen to this? Haven't I been beaten up? Don't I need to go to hospital? Please, lift me into the ambulance"

"He came to you the next morning and you convinced him that he should deny meeting Wycherley that night. He should say that he wasn't even at the Palfreyman. You knew that his alibi would be easily broken. After all, he was the man who ran downstairs, shouting murder. But you wanted him to be caught lying so that people would suspect him of the murder."

She nodded again at the orderlies and they lifted her into the back of the ambulance.

"You made one important slip, Elsie. You said that Wycherley had taken the cathedral cat to the Palfreyman, that night. Rosie, Mrs Ritchers, Mike the mechanic – they'll all say that was nonsense."

"Well, I wouldn't know, would I? I wasn't there, PC Machray, was I?"

I stopped them closing the doors.

"But you were. You were on the stairs and heard Mrs Ritchers say 'put your cat down'."

"There, so the cat was there."

"But Mrs Ritchers said, 'put your hat down'. He had ordered a tray of beer and she didn't think he'd be able to carry it with his big floppy black hat still in his hand. Only someone who was there could have misheard her, Elsie."

"Well, well, well," she said with a lazy smile. "Now there's a curiosity. I'll be hanged by the church cat. Do you think that will get me into heaven, Ned?"

Then the orderlies checked with me, I nodded and they closed her in.

I stood with the Commodore in the middle of the road. "Rosie was already working for you when she found the Captain and Elsie in a back alley," I said. "He'd drunk himself senseless and Elsie was stealing everything he'd got from the settling rooms that morning. Eighty pounds, Commodore. Much more than any man sensibly carries in his pockets."

"Three months pay to the skipper of the Tra'Lee," he agreed.

"But Elsie was very quick to think things through," I continued. "And very clever. She convinced Rosie to take sixty pounds, keeping only twenty for herself. Do you see the cleverness of that? If ever the women were found out, the Captain would judge that Rosie was the instigator because she had most of the money. That's why Irish Dowell always believed that Rosie was the thief."

Both medics sat in the front cab so Elsie was alone when they reversed over the cobbles. I heard the casualty chair crash against the sides of the vehicle as the driver turned around and accelerated towards Goodladies Road.

"I need to make sure that she's arrested," said the Commodore. He patted me on the shoulder, then marched along the close in an unhurried, well-mannered way. Authority lay lightly with the Commodore. I watched him confer with the constable at the crossroads who didn't know whether to keep to his post or make for the telephone box. At the Commodore's suggestion, he beckoned his colleague from Annie's front door. As soon as that pavement was vacated, the thin little woman slipped out of her house, climbed over the graveyard wall and followed me back to the stone bench.

I said, "She murdered him, Annie."

"I know," she said. "Did she admit it to you?"

I shook my head. "I hope she will."

"Why'd she do it, Mr Ned?"

"She was scared of what her lover would do when he found out that she had robbed him."

"Oh, jolly right too," she said, nodding like a toy doll. "We've seen that tonight, haven't we? Her face was in a terrible state." Then a puzzle look came over her face. "But why Wycherley?"

"Because she didn't want Wycherley to buy Rosie Ditchen's dog."

She needed a few seconds to understand me. She looked anxiously at the front doors of the almshouses, fifty yards away. "The old man gets cross when I'm seen out in my nightdress and no slippers." she said. "Is that what Bert was going to do? I thought he was against the dog fighting."

"That's what we all thought."

"Oh, I see. Wycherley was going to give money to Rosie ..."

"... for the dog .."

"... and Rosie was going to repay the Captain and explain that Elsie was the real thief. Ooh, yes." Annie was nodding again. "He'd have beaten her badly for that." She studied my expression. Her face was pale and twitchy. "You're very clever," she said. "You worked it out where others couldn't."

Mrs Ankers was on her feet and backing away. When she heard the Commodore approach from the iron gates, she turned and ran.

"Originally, Rosie was ready to take the money from the robbery," I explained to him. "You wanted her to get close to the dogs, so she needed to buy a Staffs Terrier. She knew that would introduce her to the family in Blackamore Lane and the old army scout in the Hoboken Arms."

He agreed. "At first, we didn't know that she'd bought a dog. She was working well for us and we gave her a free hand. She discovered good information about the watchers along the coast."

I nodded. "And they were working for Turncott, of course. They were desperate to know what Wycherley had discovered."

"Vital to an enemy, of course."

"But all the time, Elsie was intimidating Rosie. She was always scared of the Captain's violence and she needed to be sure of Rosie's silence. So she had to keep pressing her."

"Bullying her."

"Like you said, Rosie's life was full of secrets and that side of Rosie's character frightened Elsie."

The Commodore was ahead of my story. "So that's why Rosie stopped working for us. It got too much for her."

"Then she decided to sell the dog. Hubert Wycherley had been researching the coast and came across the dog fighting pit by accident. Far from wanting to stop the sport, as Elsie wanted everyone to believe, he wanted to take part. The old scout put him in touch with Rosie but Elsie got to hear about it. She realised that Rosie was backing out. She'd stopped working for you, she was giving up the dogs, the next step – Elsie feared – would be to give the Captain his money back and tell him the truth. Elsie knew that Wycherley would be the source for that money so she wanted to cut it off."

We had walked to the crossroads where, standing in the middle of the road, I said, "Then, two hours before the Wycherley murder, Irish visited his cottage in the close. They talked about poor Polly's nonsense murder but Elsie thought that she was telling him about the robbery. That made the Dean's Clerk even more of a threat. If Elsie had any doubts in her head, Irish Dowell's shape at the window convinced her that Wycherley had to be killed."

SIXTEEN

The Cobwebs Remain

They gave the case to Gutterman. After all, he had been the first detective on the scene of the murder. I reported to a cold writing room in the basement of police headquarters where I told my story three times to two inspectors. They shared it all with the Head of CID who preferred that I didn't make a statement. "All you have done, young Machray, is report the facts that Gutterman will find in his own investigation. Placing you in the enquiry would only complicate the business. You do see that, don't you?"

Gutterman wasn't there and he didn't speak to me later.

As I was leaving the scribe's room, the local inspector threw me a set of house keys. "I picked them up from Ditchen's hospital locker, two days ago. She'd like us to check on the property while she's sick. You can do it on the way home."

* * *

The house smelt damp, the kitchen tasted stale and the lights sparked and flickered as if dust had got to the electrics. For some reason that I couldn't explain, I tried all the taps in the house. One above the outside sink was stiff and, when I got it going, the back door shook in its frame. All the water was cold. I checked upstairs, avoiding the bedroom where Turncott had died because the blood would still be on the walls, floor and ceiling and I didn't want to see it. Then I turned off all the lights and sat on the back step for twenty minutes. The seat of my trousers had got caught between my legs, so I fidgeted to straighten it. "Oi! You with your hand up your arse!" someone shouted from a window. (I knew better than to look up.) I was supposed to sleep in Elsie's house, that's where I had my digs, but it didn't seem right. I had just got her arrested for murder so how could I spend the night beneath her roof? Also, I thought the CID men might be there, searching for clues in Elsie's belongings. Searching my stuff, probably.

I knew that I couldn't go back. I was supposed to be moving to the Hoboken but that wasn't settled. So, I had nowhere else to go, and no-one was here to stop me sleeping in Rosie's house. I put a kettle on the gas and found some Bournvita crystals beneath the sink. I took down the blanket that served as a curtain on the back of the front door and made something of a camp on Rosie's settee. I already had my tie off; I pulled my shirt tails from the waist band, unbuttoned my flies and lay down, exhausted. But I had hardly got comfy when someone knocked on the door.

"I saw you," said Annie.

"I was straightening myself," I said.

She didn't understand that, so I guessed that she wasn't the woman who had shouted about my backside.

"You let yourself in with a key."

"Rosie gave it to my inspector. She'd like us to keep an eye on the place."

"I'll come in then," she said. 'Coming in' wasn't easy because she was towing a handcart made from an orange box and pram wheels. "The children in Harold Street saw me struggling with a few things from your room so they said I could borrow this. I haven't got to take it back until morning."

"You've been to Elsie's place?"

"The detectives didn't mind me taking some of your clothes, night things and the sort. I thought you would be at the Hoboken but I saw you letting yourself in here."

She held back the first of her tears. "And I won't be able to sleep tonight. I – just – need to be with you."

"That's nonsense, Annie. You've got Josh."

We left the cart at the bottom of the stairs and I followed her into the parlour.

"Please, don't be grouchy with me. Not tonight," she said. "God,

145

do you realise what we've done? We've put Elsie in gaol and she's probably going to hang. God, Ned, do you think they'll do it to her?"

"Come on," I said, not answering. "We should be able to find something to eat." I went into the kitchen and opened some cupboards. She leant against the doorframe and said, "You worked it out, didn't you, like a Sherlock Holmes?"

I wasn't looking at her. I was too busy searching Rosie's pantry. "Oh, dear little Annie, do stop pretending. You knew that it was Elsie. From the beginning, you knew."

"Not from the beginning," she insisted. "But I solved your riddle-me-ree pretty easily. I wasn't going to confess, so it wasn't me. Rosie's sense of justice – well, she could put things right with money. She just had to pay the Captain. She didn't have to kill anyone. But Elsie, yes, she was a bully. And I've surely learned that bullies don't need a reason to do anything. Well, not much of one." She gave me an adoring smile, I thought. "Of course, you were much more clever than I was. I really thought that I was to blame, saying that I'd seen Irish and Hubert together at the window."

"No, no." I assured her, "Elsie had already decided to kill him. She's made a statement agreeing that everything was just as I said." I laid a patronising hand on her shoulder. "Besides, Wycherley and Miss Dowell weren't talking about the stolen money."

"Oh, no. It was the other murder, you said."

* * *

Cobwebs at the corners of Rosie's bedroom ceiling were wafting in a draft and I couldn't work it out. The bedroom door was closed and Annie had laid a woolly sausage at the bottom. I had already noticed that the windows were sealed with putty. But still there was a draft.

"It must be the chimney," Annie said softly. "You puzzle over too many things, you know." She shook her head in mock despair. "You worry, you do."

I didn't say anything.

"Was it very horrible?" she whispered.

"Not at all."

146

"That's because you couldn't see me properly."

"Don't be silly, Annie."

She waited, then asked, "I'm very ugly, aren't I?"

I was twenty-seven but much younger; Annie was forty-two yet older. The idle calculation – I was looking up at the ceiling while her head was laid on my chest, her mouth going 'pit-pit-pit' at my hairs too close to her face – reinforced the truth that I was in bed with a woman old enough to be my mother. That's nothing wrong, I told myself. You'd make nothing of it, young Ned, if an older man was with a young lady.

She sensed that I wanted to disturb the peace of our lying together. "We don't have to leave each other for hours. Josh'll be back from his poaching but he won't shout for me and he never comes into my bedroom, you must have worked that out. He'll leave for work at five and not even know that I'm out of the house." She reached for the bag at the bedside and produced two cigarettes. It was a brand for girls but I took one. She lit both at once with no trouble then laid her head of scraggly hair on my chest again. She blew smoke towards my neck.

I could tell that she wanted to talk so I asked, "Can you sing?"

She sniggered. "You wouldn't want me to try."

"I was thinking of your nickname. Annie 'Canary'."

"I was Annie Cannary at school, wasn't I?" she explained patiently. "We've said all this. Cannary the Canary went well together, didn't it? Now, stop bothering about things."

"Cannary? Where does that come from? Ireland?"

She took her time. "America. My mother was a twin; I've told you that, haven't I? Well, she was adopted. I mean, the two sisters were separated and placed with different families. It was strange because they were both called Janey, although they didn't know about each other, of course. My mum only found out later, when her older cousins told her. That was when she was dying, wasn't it? And then they told me. One sister – she'd be my aunt, wouldn't she? – she stayed in America and the other Janey – my mum – came to England. Her adopted father was a sea captain in the China Sea, Mum always said. At first, she wasn't Cannary but the family told her before she got married; except she didn't get married in the end because it all

147

sent her a bit queer. But she still had me and then she learned about the other Janey when she was sick. Shame, don't you think? A bit sad, really."

She thought for a few moments, then said, "He couldn't have been a captain in the China Sea. I remember a picture of his boat and my mother said it was full of people going to America. So it couldn't have been, could it? China, I mean. Now, turn the other way. I want to use the pot and it's too cold to go downstairs."

We both got up and I sat on the edge of the mattress while she busied herself round the other side of the bed. "Annie," I asked. "Everything turned out right, didn't it? I mean, as it should have done?"

"Oh yes. It's just like the school playground, all those years ago."

I knew that she wasn't telling me everything. She seemed too content.

"Elsie shouting at us," she continued. "Making us do things and taking our sweets. But, all the time, she was a big sister who wouldn't let Rosie and me get into trouble."

That new aeroplane was night flying again. Its engine sounded so slow and popping that I wondered how it stayed in the air. The pilot kept it over the city for forty minutes, circling then cutting across. At first, I thought he was photographing the geography of our town but he couldn't do that in the night. Finally, he came in alarmingly low. His wings seesawed over the cathedral. It was as if he was trying to frighten us all before he rose above the smoky coloured clouds in the night sky and flew away. His signature grew quieter and more distant. Then there was noise from a freighter leaving the harbour and a goods train shunting in the railway yard.

I turned to face her. "This town seems so nervy, it worries me," I said, not knowing what she would make of it. "I've only been here for six months and I can't settle to anything. I can't concentrate. I can't, I don't know, I can't accept things."

She knew what I meant. "It's like we can't sit down for too long. I know, I'm just the same."

We clambered back into bed and cuddled up. She whispered, "What I want to know is ..." She laid her face on my chest, collected two hairs between her teeth and gave a playful tug. "... How did you escape from Polly's attic?"

I whimpered and she let go. "It was the dog that saved me," I confessed. "I'd got Polly ready for prayers when her father and his terrier crashed into the room. The dog was sure that I was about to do something peculiar and jumped between us to protect the girl. He was snarling and spitting, gnashing his teeth. Saliva was everywhere. I couldn't get near poor Polly again."

"How peculiar?"

"Very," I agreed. "Well, her father forgot about the blackmail and chased me down the stairs. If the dog wanted to fight me, he shouted, I was too much of a scoundrel to mess with his daughter."

"How peculiar?"

"Damned peculiar."

"No," Annie persisted. "I mean, how were you going to do something peculiar?"

I knew she was only teasing.[7]

* * *

This mystery of cross women has one further postscript. On 17 May 1953, Rosie Ditchen was hanged for the murder of Louis Bloire twenty years before. She had been a kitchen maid at his school where she told lies to get him a beating. She was allowed to observe the punishment and, afterwards, she told another domestic that the pain on the boy's face thrilled her more than any other image. Later, Bloire came to our city seeking confrontation and Rosie stabbed him in his heart. She said that he attacked her and fell on his own knife and most people thought that the jury would believe her. But they were against her. The story of the school beating had cast her as a cruel and sadistic spinster. She claimed he had sewn a special pocket into the lining of his jacket so that he could carry a knife. David Tupner and I gave evidence, describing the jacket, but it sounded weak and the jacket couldn't be found after all that time. Rosie had

---

7 At the time, I paid no attention to Annie's ideas about her grandfather. When, twenty years later, Soapy Berkeley explained the significance of her family legend, it was too late to ask Annie for proof or more details. Honestly, I don't think she realised what people would make of it. She was simply repeating what her cousins had told her. But who knows? It may be that, on an arresting night in 1937, I bedded an unacknowledged grand-daughter of Calamity Jane and Wild Bill Hickok.

arranged for the body to be dumped at sea and, when she heard that Bloire had prayed for poor Polly in her loft, she paid the father five pounds to put gossip around that he had killed the young man. He complained that it was a mean amount. "Don't worry. No-one will believe it in court," Rosie said.

I was standing on the concourse of Kings Cross when I read the headline. I remembered Elsie's judgement that Rosie could commit murder for the sake of justice. Now, she had been condemned by a trial which had little to do with fairness. That's what I thought. I wanted to blame someone, so I went to one of the brown wooden phone boxes with sliding doors and rang the Commodore. I didn't need to introduce myself. "I thought we didn't hang people because they were the wrong sort," I snarled and put the phone down. That told him. I went through the barrier, stowed my luggage above a first class seat and stepped out to the platform for a smoke.

I remembered Annie's picture of three girls in a playground, with Elsie acting like a big sister, doing anything to keep Rosie out of trouble. Perhaps, after all, she had needed to stop Wycherley talking about the Blackamore Lane murder. Had the three women been working together? Elsie the bully, Rosie who wanted to make up for mistakes and Annie who always told the truth. I was sure that Annie was no killer but she certainly knew more than she told. Throughout that week in 1937, Annie had carefully dropped clues for me to pick up, so what had been her part in any intrigue?

"Are you travelling, sir?" asked a porter at my shoulder.

"To tell the truth," I said absently.

"Sir?"

I looked up. Rain and mist promised a miserable journey north. I trod my cigarette into the ground and climbed aboard. As I took my seat, I was pleased to see that a vicar was my only travelling companion. Reverends, I have found, know when to keep quiet and I was in no mood for bothersome company.

The murder in the Palfreyman was an old case. It was 'pre-war' and, in the 1950s, there was a feeling that we should move on from old things. Wycherley was dead; Rosie and Elsie had been dispatched. There were no families to mourn them, so who cared why an old Dean's Clerk died?

I said to myself, "In the end, she was a good girl."

"I think so," said the vicar as he closed the last page of his Agatha Christie. He placed it with two others on the empty seat beside him. "But I always suspected her from Chapter Two."

He picked up the next book, smiled as he prepared to lose himself in page one, and the train went into a tunnel.

THE TIMBERDICK MYSTERIES

"Noble has a fine knack of creating a sense of place and atmosphere. He has created an intriguing set of characters." (Portsmouth Post)

"A marvellous creation. Noble reels off a first rate story. Vastly entertaining" (Nottingham Post)

"He leaves you begging for the next in the series." (Montgomeryshire Advertiser)

TIMBERDICK'S FIRST CASE
Matador Paperback
ISBN 1-904744-33-8

Timberdick worked the pavements of Goodladies Road where the men had bad ideas and the girls should have known better. In 1963, the murder of a prostitute challenges more than Timbers' detective skills. "Real people get murdered by their family and friends," says one of the girls. "We get killed by everyone else."

LIKING GOOD JAZZ
Matador Paperback
ISBN 1-904744-96-6

Searching for an abandoned infant, Timberdick learns that the father has been murdered. She can trust no-one, not even those who are close to her. Before it's all over, she's sure of only one thing. No place rocks like the Hoboken Arms on Tuesday night!

PIGGY TUCKER'S POISON
Matador Paperback
ISBN 1-904-905237-18-9

Timberdick is back! She's living in the vestry and working nights in the Curiosity Shop when a stranger is murdered at the top of the stairs. Timbers is arrested but she has no time to waste in a police cell. She has a murder to solve and a bun in the oven

THE CASE OF THE DIRTY VERGER
Matador Paperback
ISBN 1-905886-31-4

It's 1947 but there's still no peace of Goodladies Road. Men without a war and girls without homes is a cocktail for murder. We explore Timberdick's first nights on Goodladies Road and find clues to many of the characters that we have already met in her later cases.

THE PARISH OF FRAYED ENDS
Matador Paperback
ISBN 978-1906221-799

When the Chief Constable asks questions about a superintendent who was buried two years ago, our street-wise detective finds that she is investigating three murders instead of one. But three suspects say that they were in bed with her favourite policeman on the night of the murder, so Timbers can see only one way forward. She sets a date for her wedding.

Keep up to date with Timberdick's website
www.bookcabin.co.uk